Pokémon
SWORD & SHIELD
4

STORY
Hidenori Kusa

ART
Satoshi Yamamoto

Henry
SWORD

THE DESCENDANT OF A RENOWNED SWORDSMITH, HENRY IS AN ARTISAN WHO FIXES AND IMPROVES POKÉMON GEAR.

Casey
SHIELD

AN ELITE HACKER AND COMPUTER TECH WHO CAN ACCESS ANY DATA SHE WANTS. SHE'S PROFESSOR MAGNOLIA'S ASSISTANT AND TEAM ANALYST.

The Story So Far

UPON ARRIVING IN THE GALAR REGION, MARVIN SEES A DYNAMAXED POKÉMON AND FALLS OFF A CLIFF! HE IS SAVED BY HENRY SWORD AND CASEY SHIELD, AND JOINS THEM ON THEIR JOURNEY TO DISCOVER THE SECRET OF DYNAMAXING WITH PROFESSOR MAGNOLIA. HENRY AND CASEY ARE ALSO BEGINNING THEIR GYM CHALLENGE! THEIR JOURNEY CONTINUES AFTER THEIR FIRST GYM BATTLE AT TURFFIELD TOWN. WHAT'S NEXT FOR THEM?

Marvin

MARVIN'S A ROOKIE TRAINER WHO RECENTLY MOVED TO GALAR. HE'S EXCITED TO LEARN EVERYTHING HE CAN ABOUT POKÉMON!

Professor Magnolia

A FAMED RESEARCHER WHO STUDIES "DYNAMAXING," A.K.A. THE GIGANTIFICATION OF POKÉMON.

Leon

LEON IS THE BEST TRAINER IN GALAR. HE'S THE UNDEFEATED CHAMPION!

Sonia

PROFESSOR MAGNOLIA'S GRANDDAUGHTER AND LEON'S CHILDHOOD FRIEND. SHE'S HELPING THE PROFESSOR INVESTIGATE THE GALAR REGION!

CONTENTS

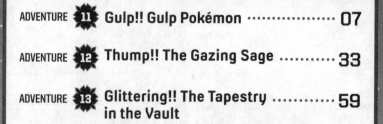

Adventure 11 Gulp!! Gulp Pokémon

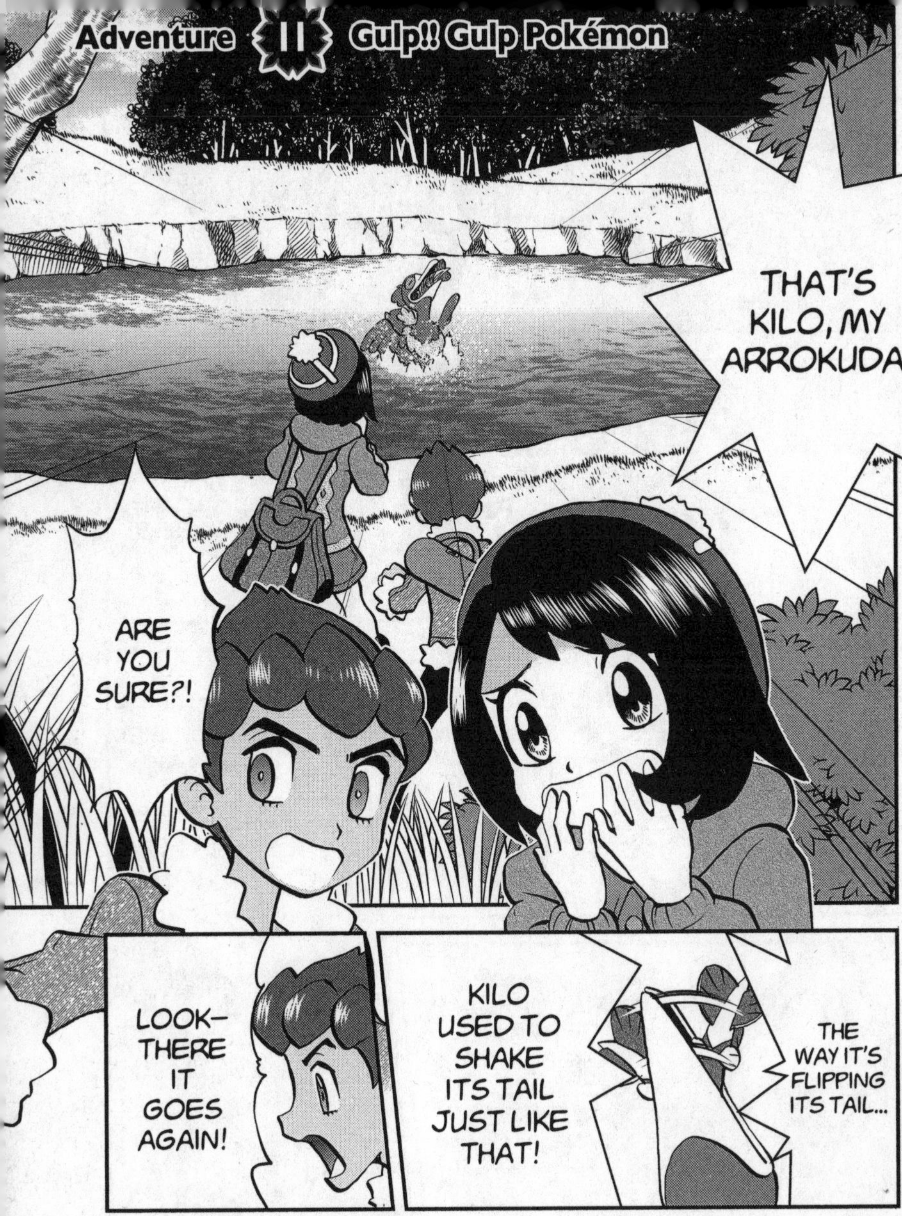
THAT'S KILO, MY ARROKUDA!
ARE YOU SURE?!
THE WAY IT'S FLIPPING ITS TAIL...
KILO USED TO SHAKE ITS TAIL JUST LIKE THAT!
LOOK—THERE IT GOES AGAIN!

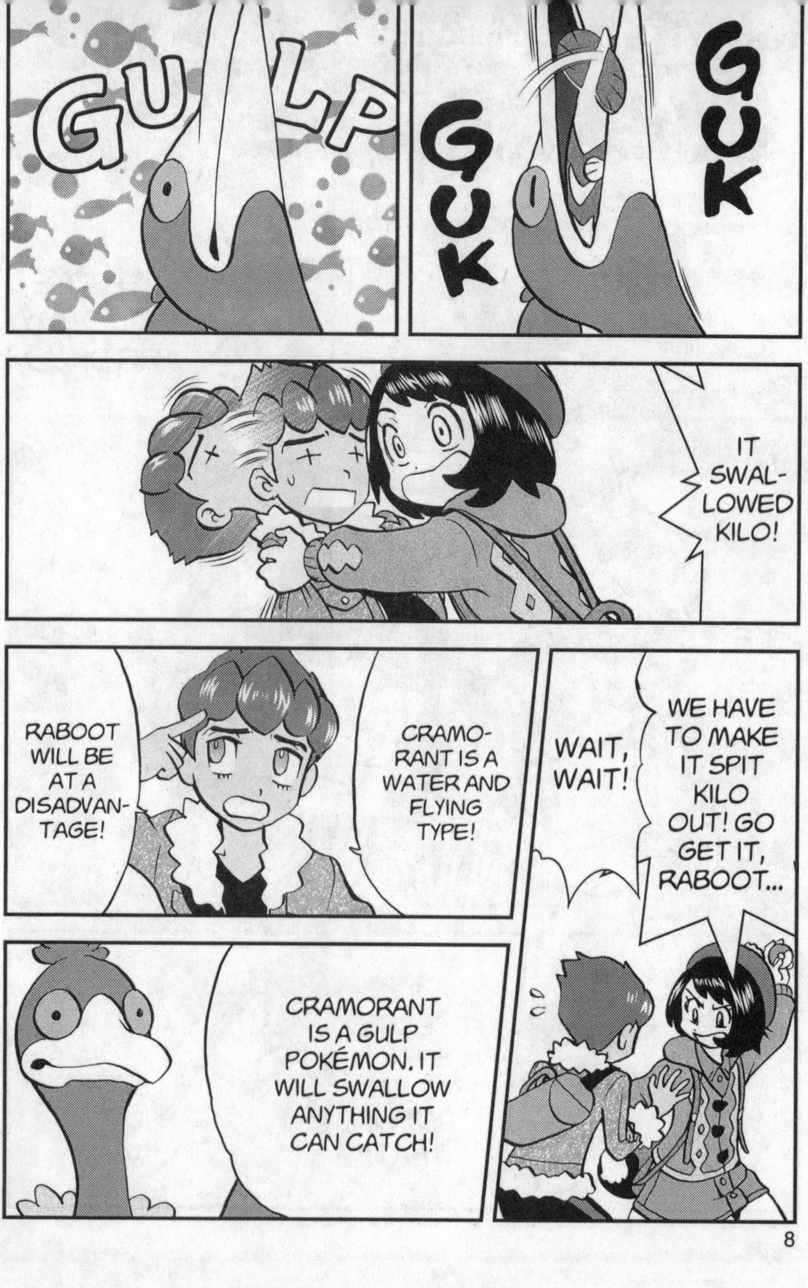
GUK
GUK
GULP
IT SWALLOWED KILO!
WE HAVE TO MAKE IT SPIT KILO OUT! GO GET IT, RABOOT...
WAIT, WAIT!
CRAMORANT IS A WATER AND FLYING TYPE!
RABOOT WILL BE AT A DISADVANTAGE!
CRAMORANT IS A GULP POKÉMON. IT WILL SWALLOW ANYTHING IT CAN CATCH!

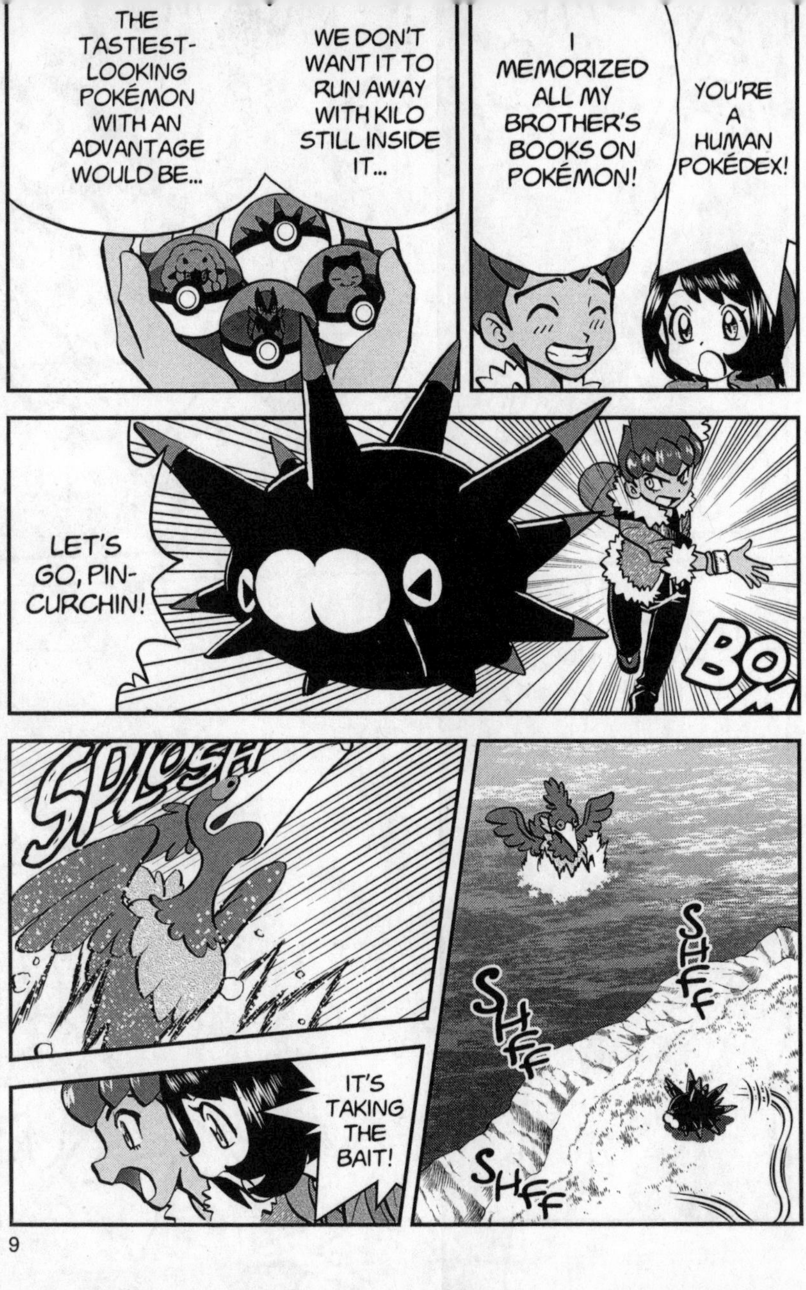
I MEMORIZED ALL MY BROTHER'S BOOKS ON POKÉMON!
YOU'RE A HUMAN POKÉDEX!
THE TASTIEST-LOOKING POKÉMON WITH AN ADVANTAGE WOULD BE...
WE DON'T WANT IT TO RUN AWAY WITH KILO STILL INSIDE IT...
BOOM
LET'S GO, PIN-CURCHIN!
SHFF
SHFF
SHFF
SPLOSH
IT'S TAKING THE BAIT!

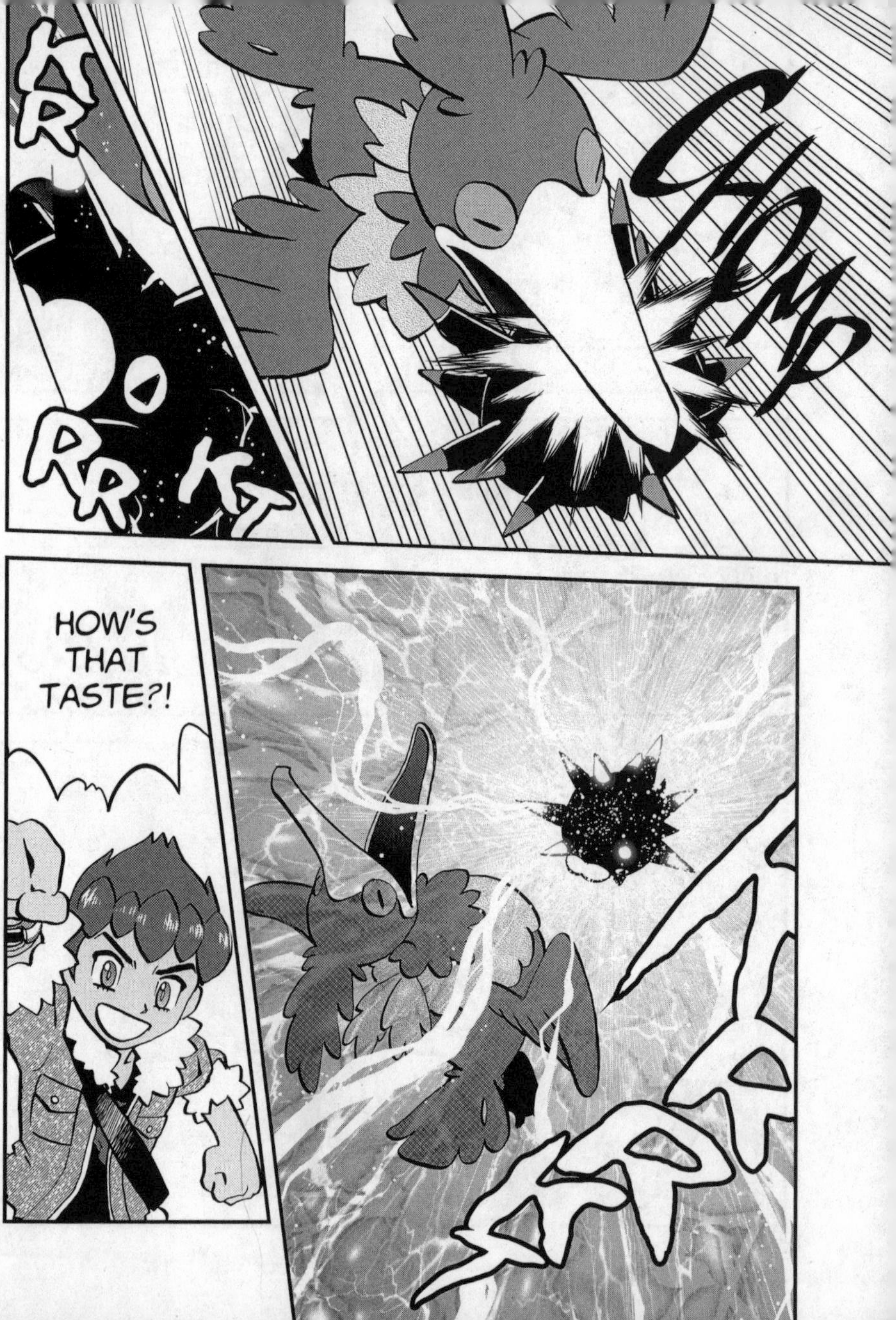
CHOMP
HOW'S THAT TASTE?!

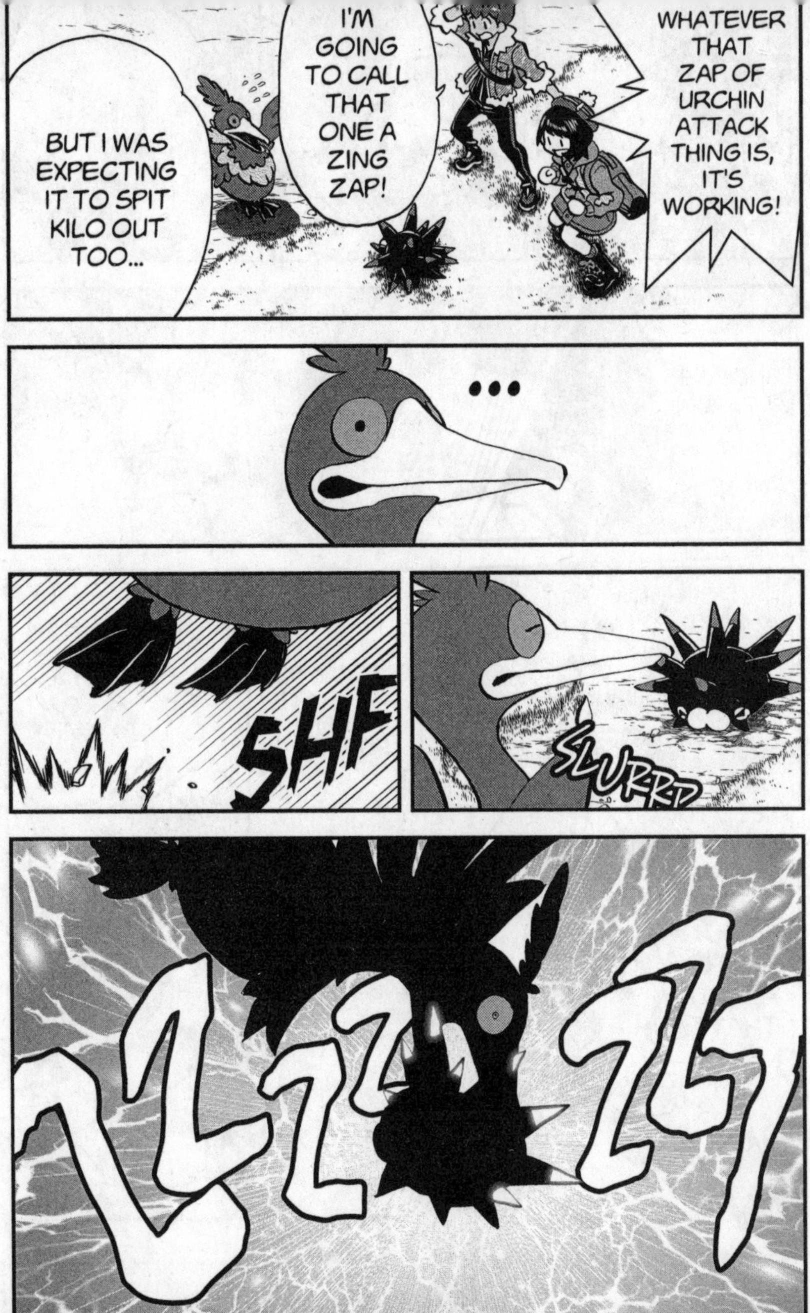
WHATEVER THAT ZAP OF URCHIN ATTACK THING IS, IT'S WORKING!
I'M GOING TO CALL THAT ONE A ZING ZAP!
BUT I WAS EXPECTING IT TO SPIT KILO OUT TOO...
...
SLURRRP
SHF
ZZZZZZT

ENOUGH ALREADY!

CHOMP

Type:	FLYING
Height:	2'07''
Weight:	39.7 lbs
Number Battled:	

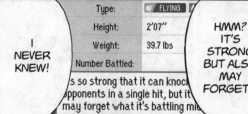

...s so strong that it can knock...
...pponents in a single hit, but it...
...may forget what it's battling mi...

I NEVER KNEW!

HMM? IT'S STRONG BUT ALSO MAY FORGET...

LOOK, HOP!

DOESN'T THIS GUY LEARN?

YOU HEARD ABOUT THAT?!

YOU USED A VIKAVOLT DRONE TO HELP HENRY DURING THE WOOLOO INCIDENT, RIGHT?

12

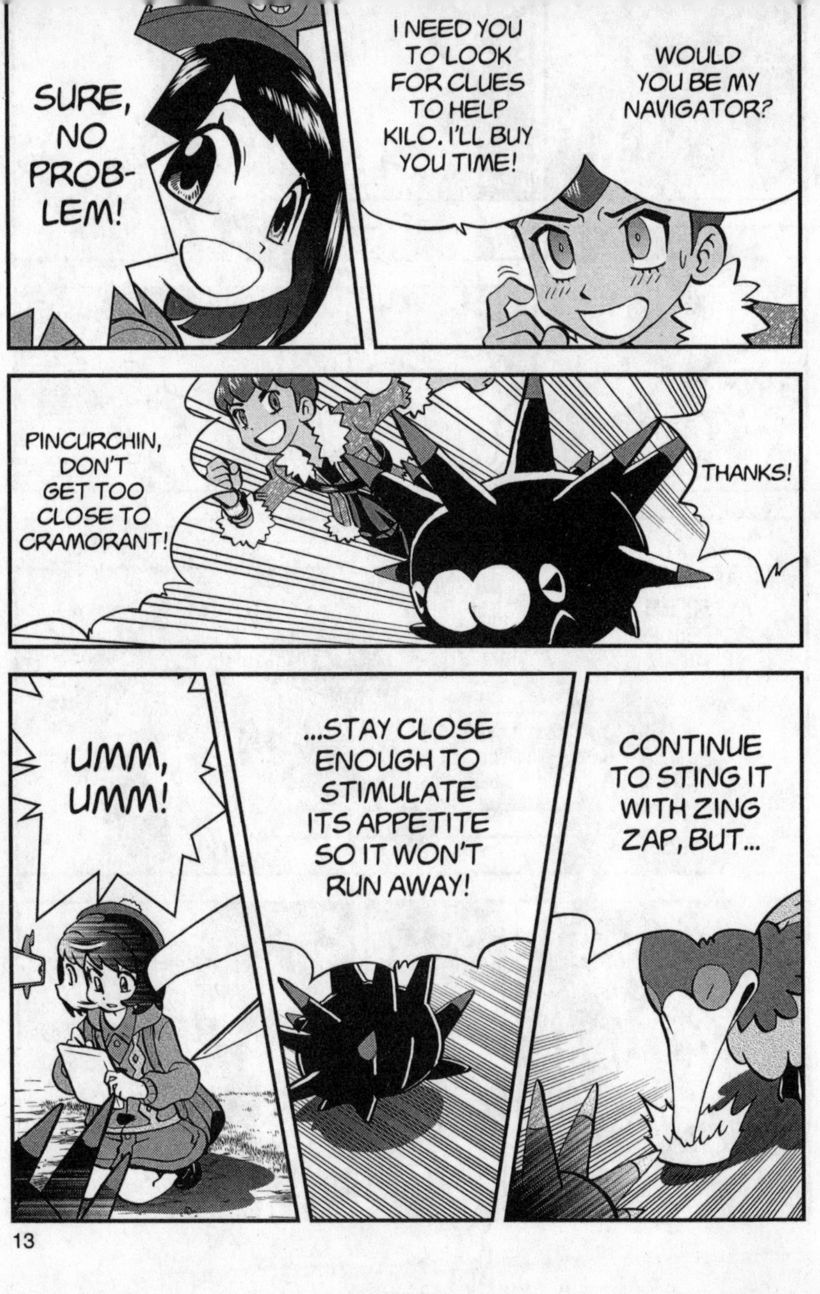
WOULD YOU BE MY NAVIGATOR?
I NEED YOU TO LOOK FOR CLUES TO HELP KILO. I'LL BUY YOU TIME!
SURE, NO PROB-LEM!
THANKS!
PINCURCHIN, DON'T GET TOO CLOSE TO CRAMORANT!
CONTINUE TO STING IT WITH ZING ZAP, BUT...
...STAY CLOSE ENOUGH TO STIMULATE ITS APPETITE SO IT WON'T RUN AWAY!
UMM, UMM!

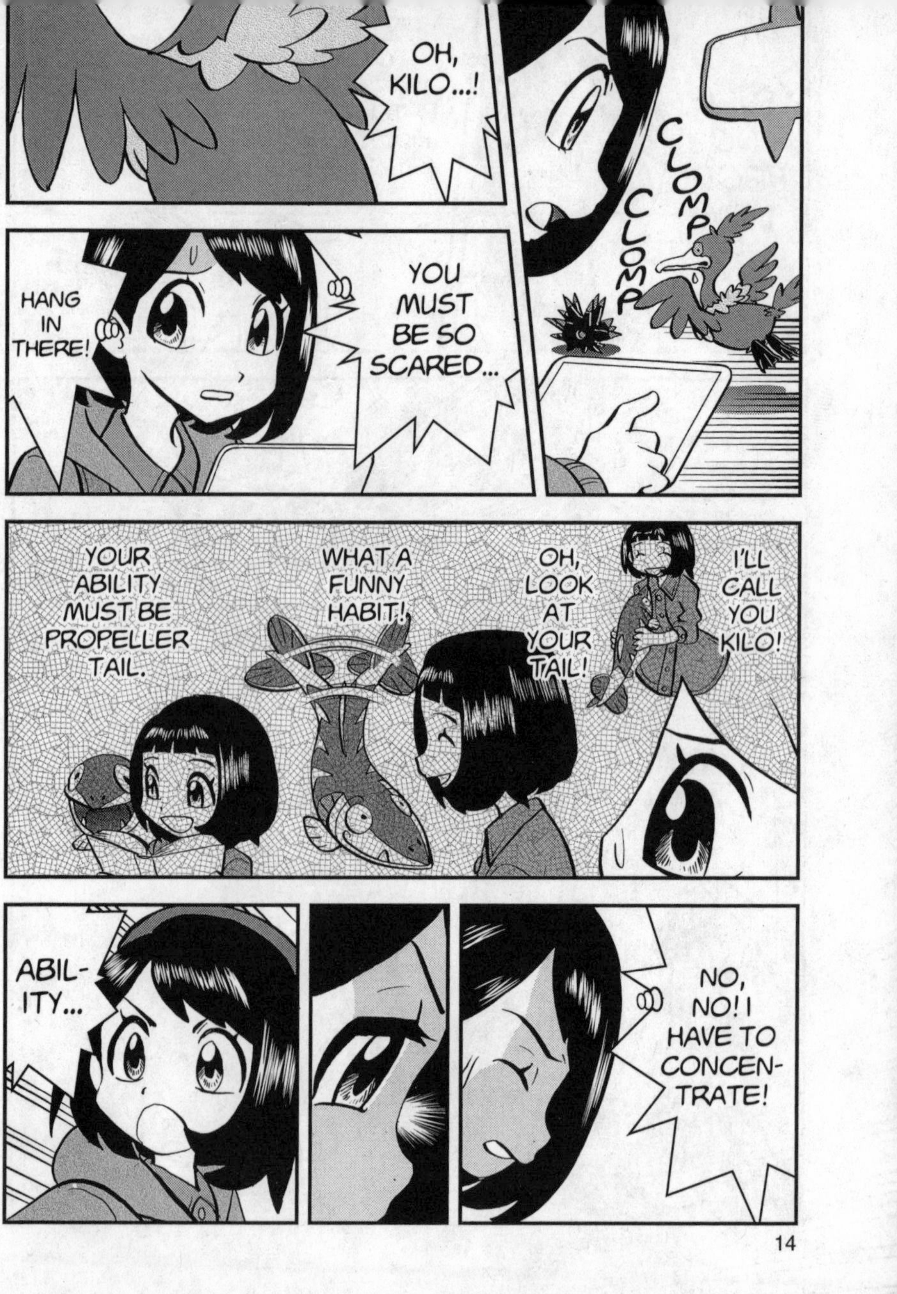
CLOMP
CLOMP
OH, KILO...!
YOU MUST BE SO SCARED...
HANG IN THERE!
I'LL CALL YOU KILO!
OH, LOOK AT YOUR TAIL!
WHAT A FUNNY HABIT!
YOUR ABILITY MUST BE PROPELLER TAIL.
NO, NO! I HAVE TO CONCEN-TRATE!
ABIL-ITY...

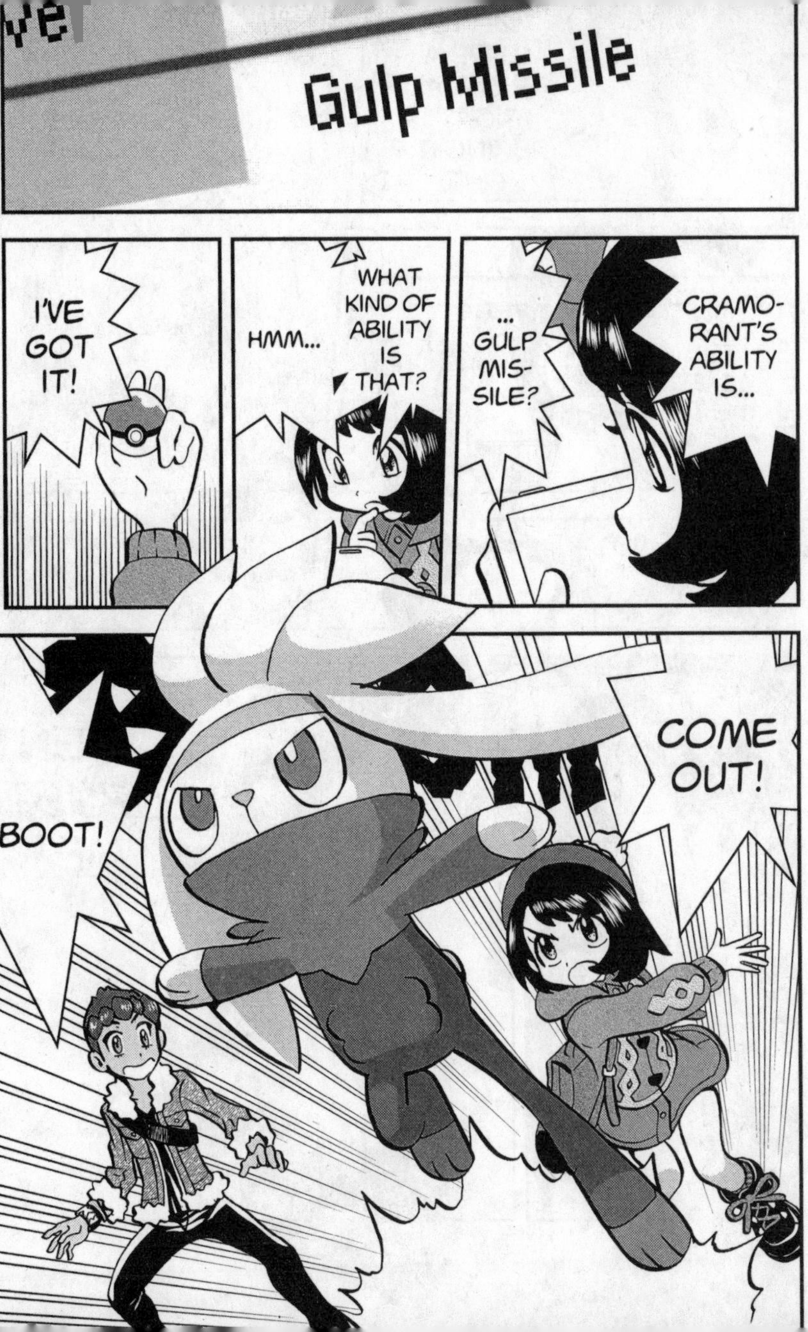
Gulp Missile
CRAMO-RANT'S ABILITY IS...
... GULP MIS-SILE?
WHAT KIND OF ABILITY IS THAT?
HMM...
I'VE GOT IT!
COME OUT!
RABOOT!

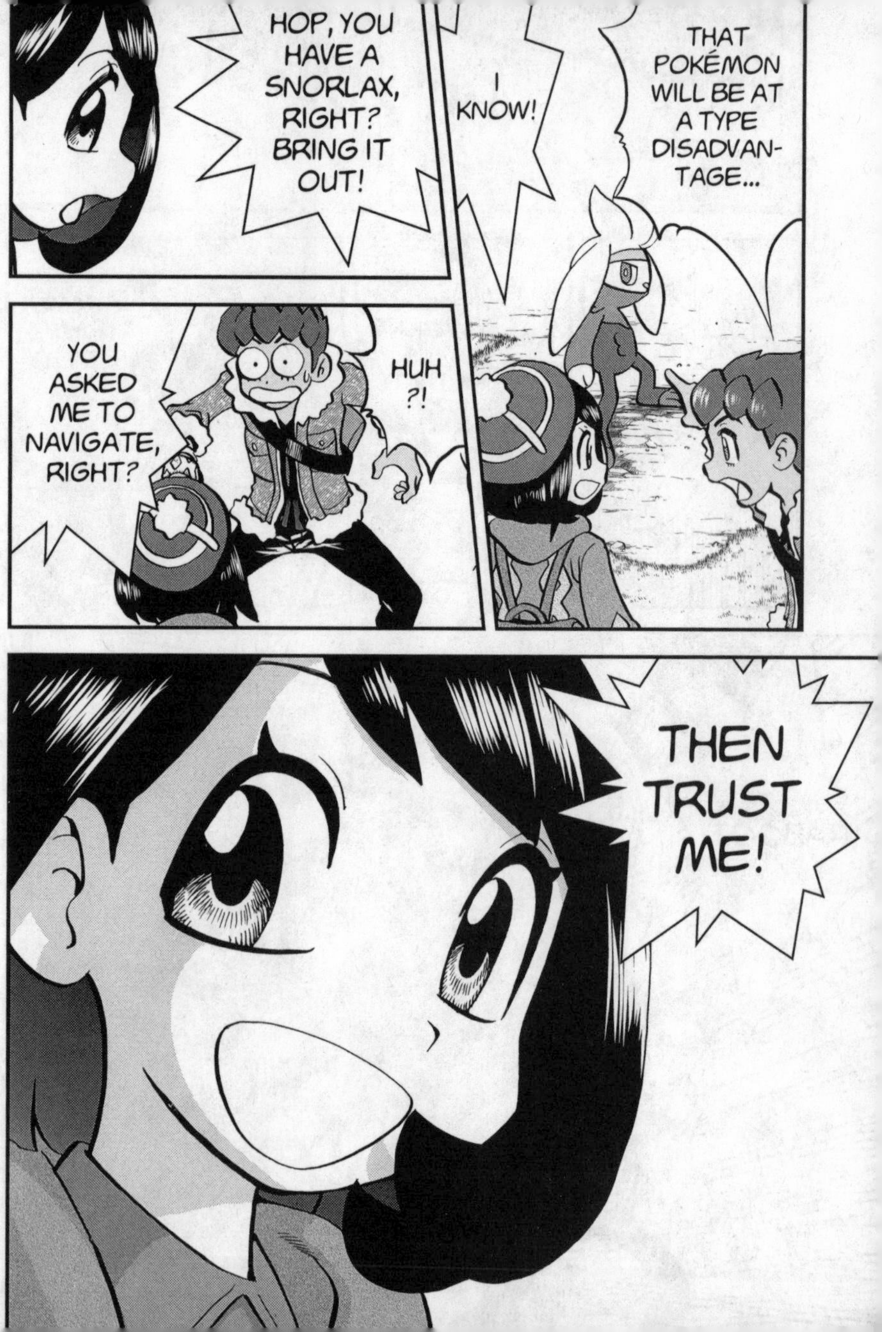
THAT POKÉMON WILL BE AT A TYPE DISADVANTAGE...
I KNOW!
HOP, YOU HAVE A SNORLAX, RIGHT? BRING IT OUT!
HUH?!
YOU ASKED ME TO NAVIGATE, RIGHT?
THEN TRUST ME!

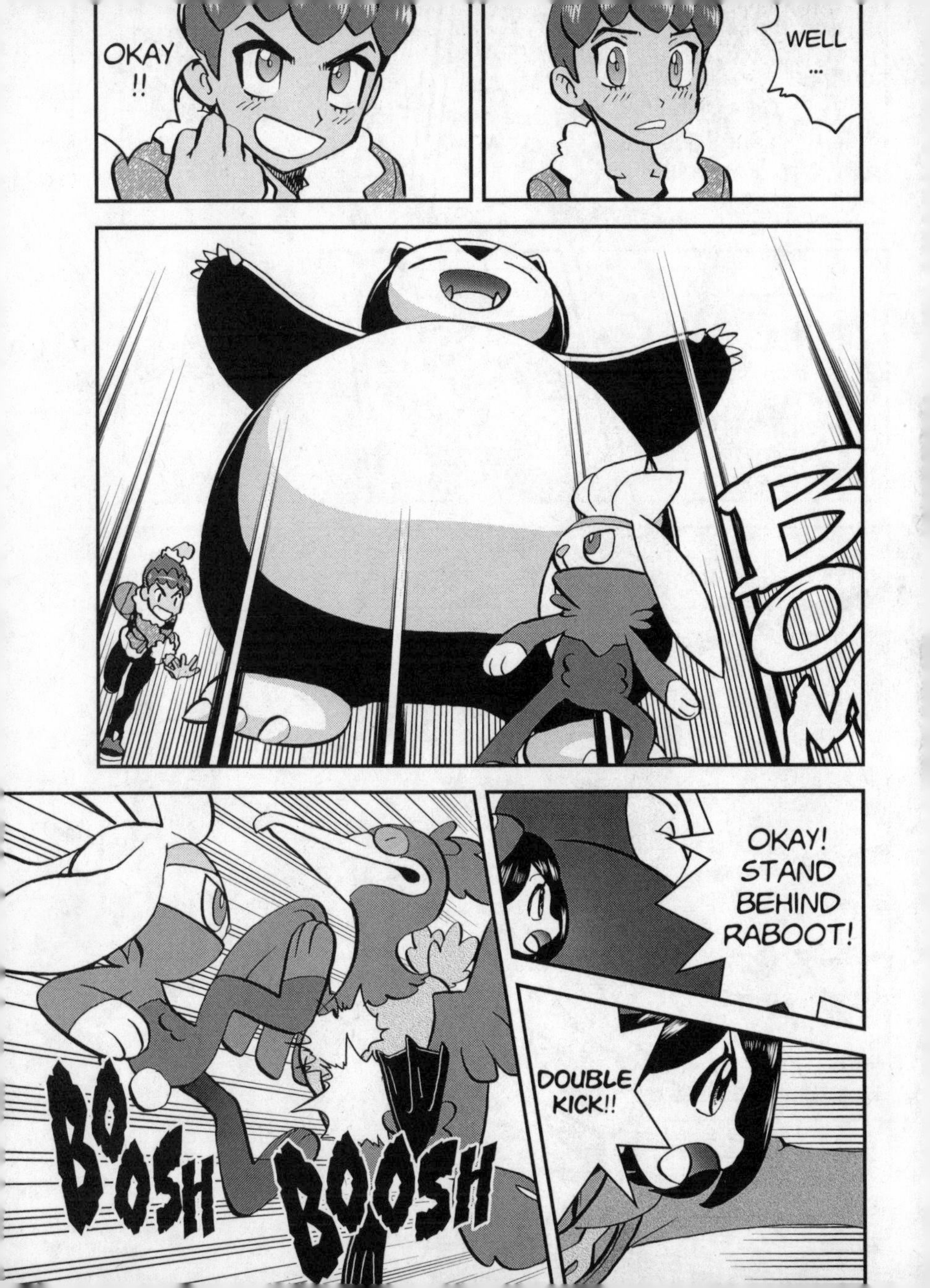
WELL ...
OKAY !!
BOOM
OKAY! STAND BEHIND RABOOT!
DOUBLE KICK!!
BOOSH
BOOSH

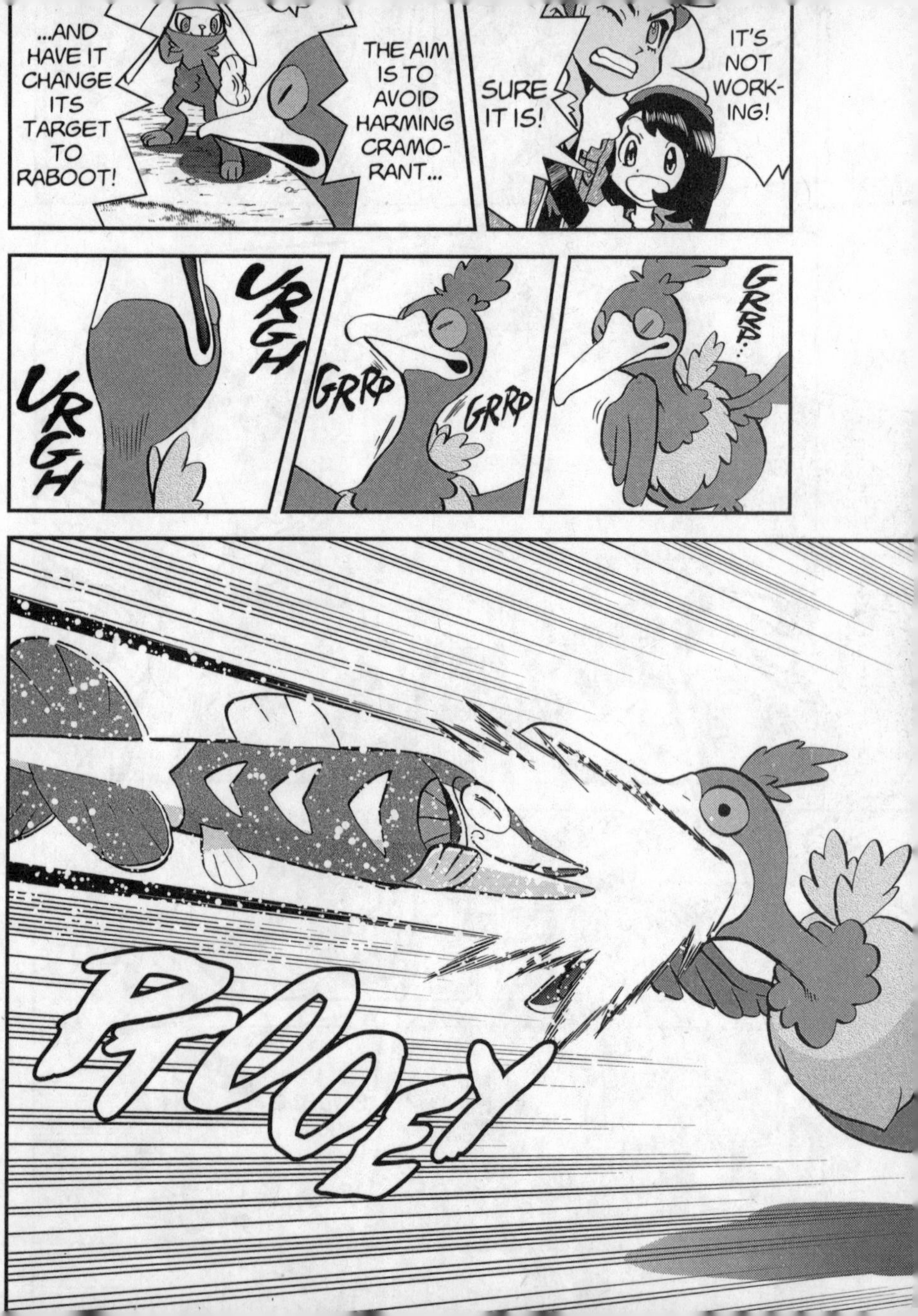

IT'S NOT WORKING!
SURE IT IS!
THE AIM IS TO AVOID HARMING CRAMORANT...
...AND HAVE IT CHANGE ITS TARGET TO RABOOT!
GRRP...
GRRP
GRRP
URGH
URGH
PTOOEY

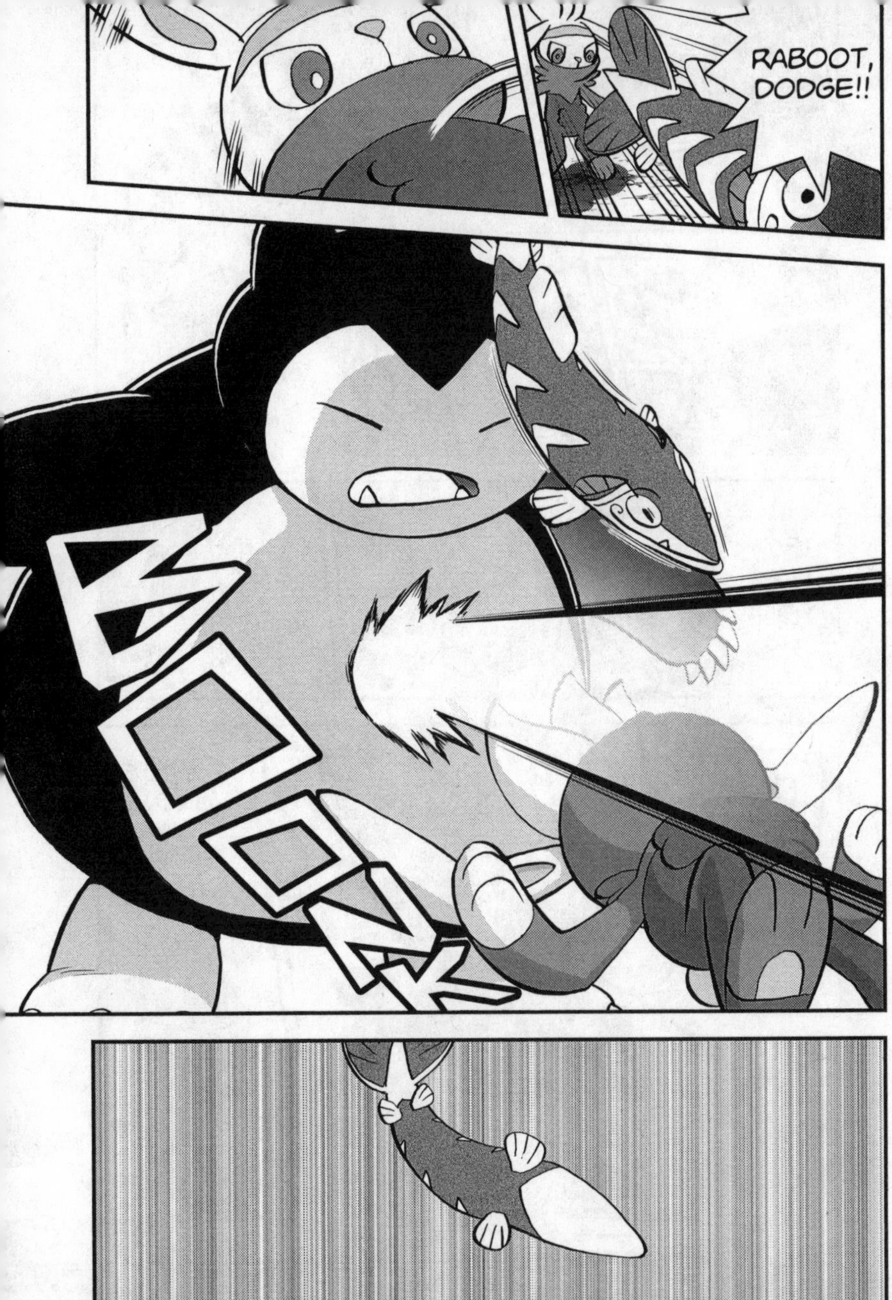
RABOOT, DODGE!!
WOONK

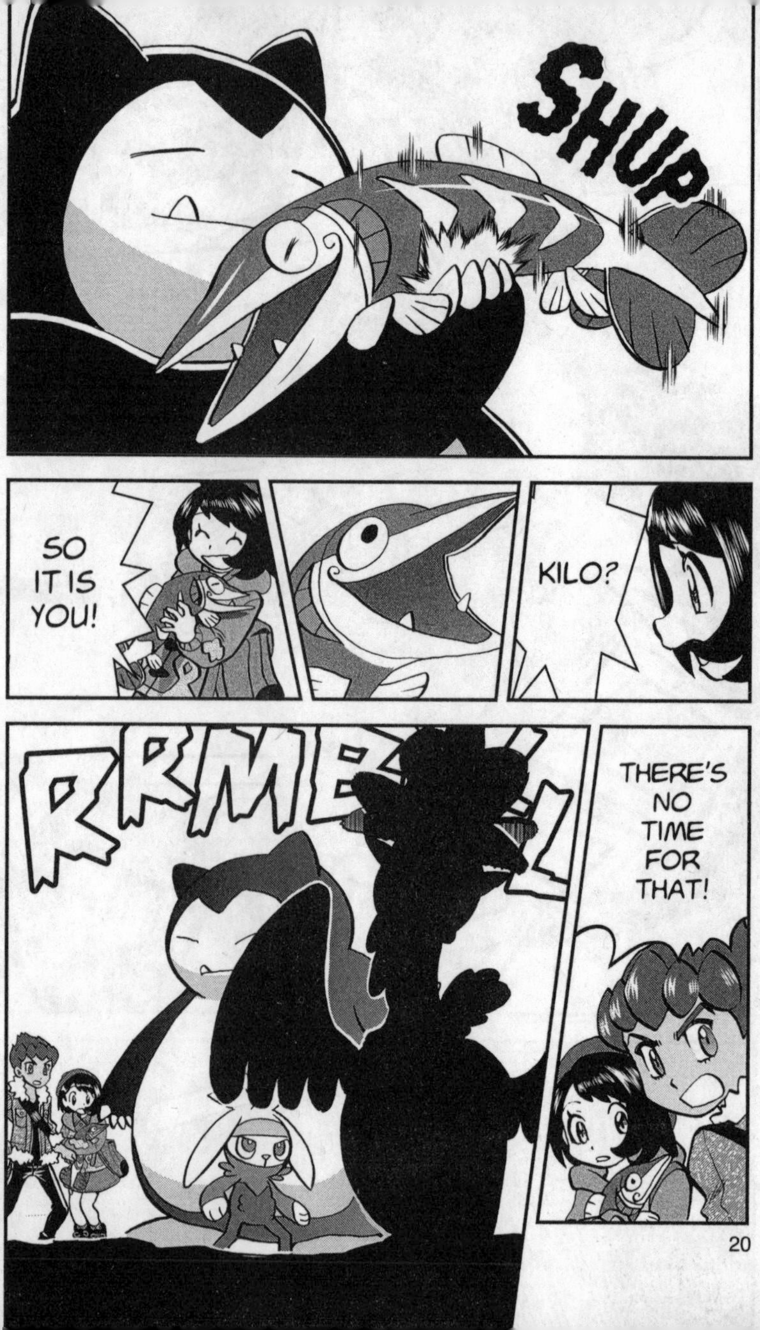
SHUP
KILO?
SO IT IS YOU!
THERE'S NO TIME FOR THAT!
RRMB

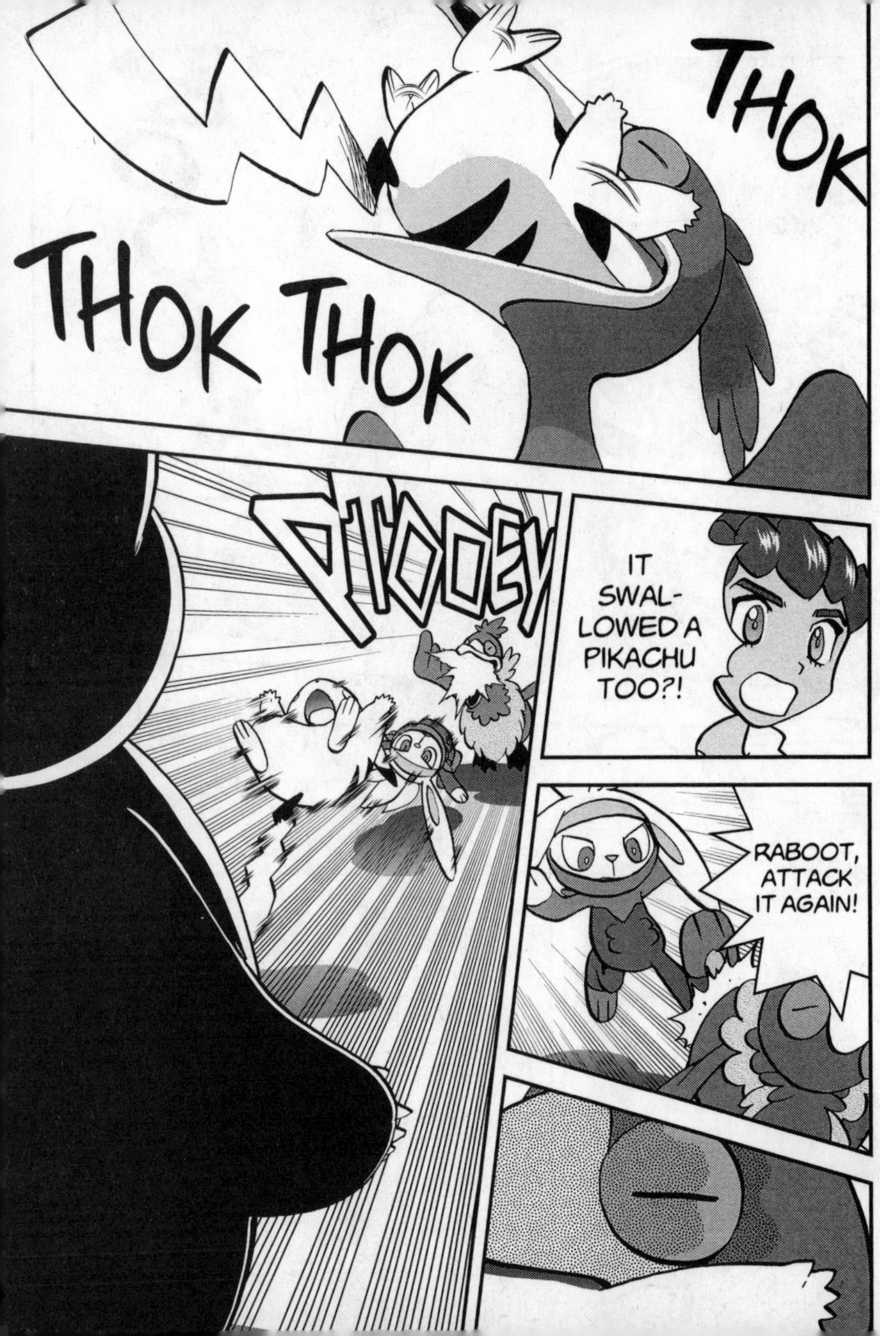
THOK
THOK THOK
IT SWALLOWED A PIKACHU TOO?!
RABOOT, ATTACK IT AGAIN!
PTOOEY

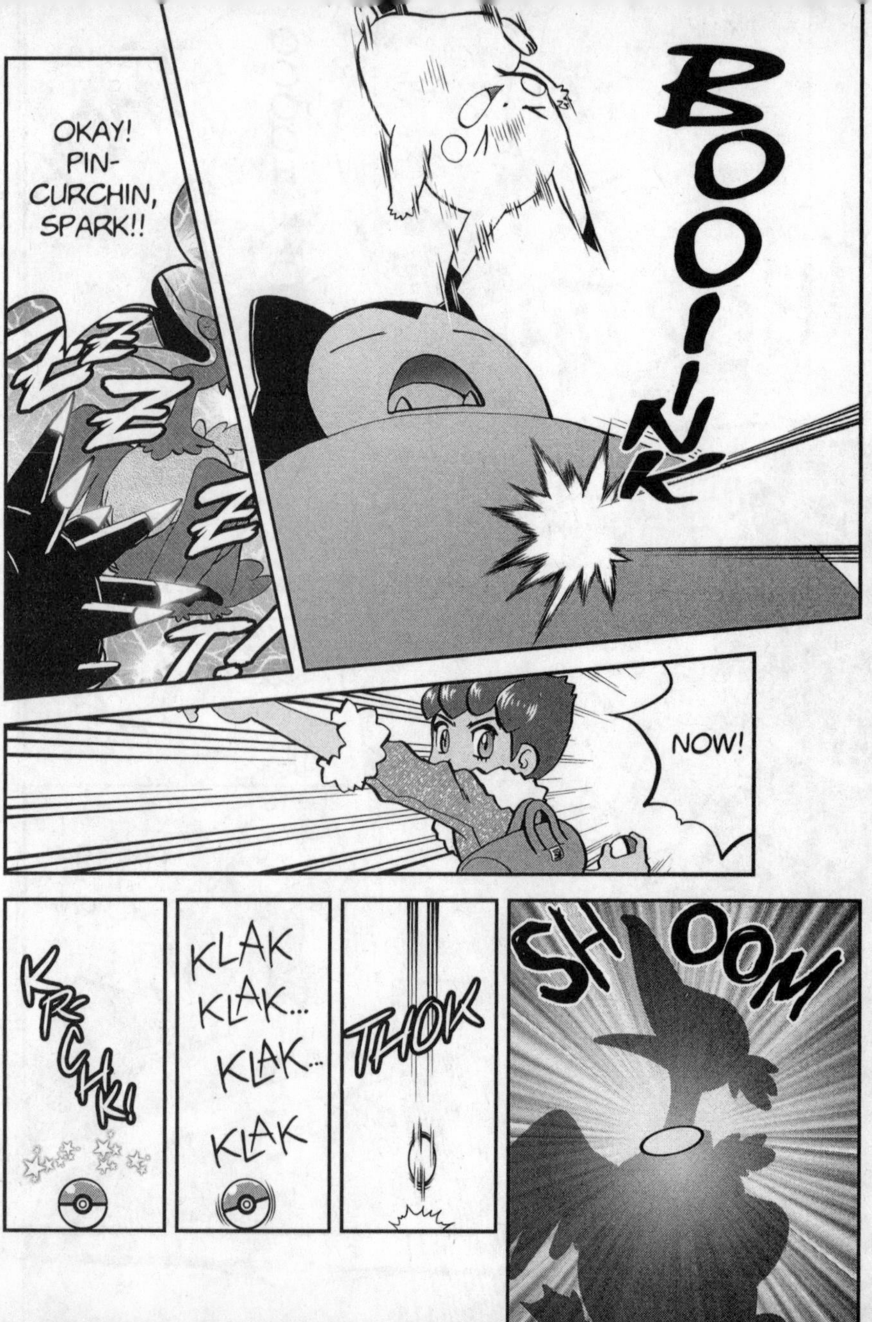
BOOOINK
OKAY! PIN-CURCHIN, SPARK!!
NOW!
SHOOM
THOK
KLAK KLAK... KLAK... KLAK
KRCHK!

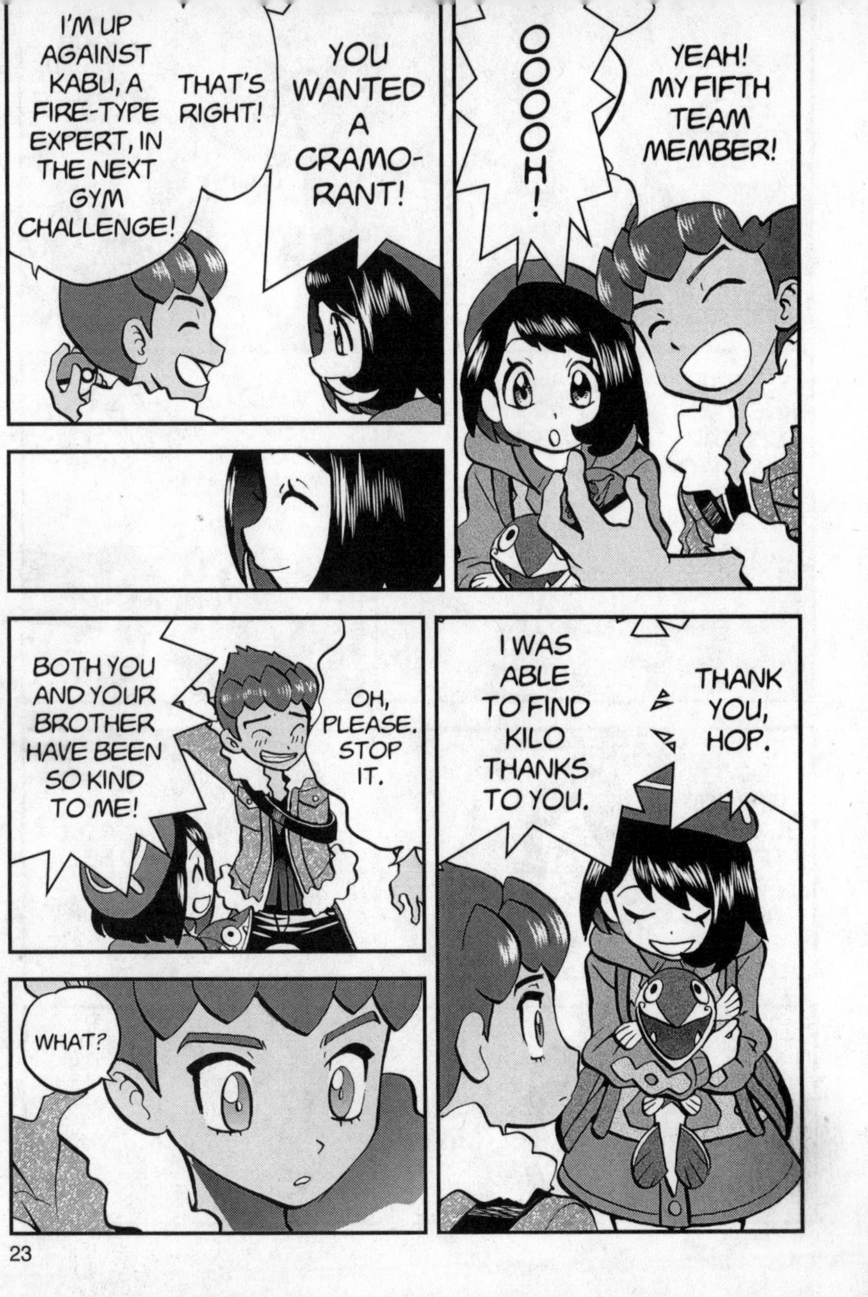
YEAH! MY FIFTH TEAM MEMBER!
OOOOOH!
YOU WANTED A CRAMO-RANT!
THAT'S RIGHT!
I'M UP AGAINST KABU, A FIRE-TYPE EXPERT, IN THE NEXT GYM CHALLENGE!
THANK YOU, HOP.
I WAS ABLE TO FIND KILO THANKS TO YOU.
OH, PLEASE. STOP IT.
BOTH YOU AND YOUR BROTHER HAVE BEEN SO KIND TO ME!
WHAT?

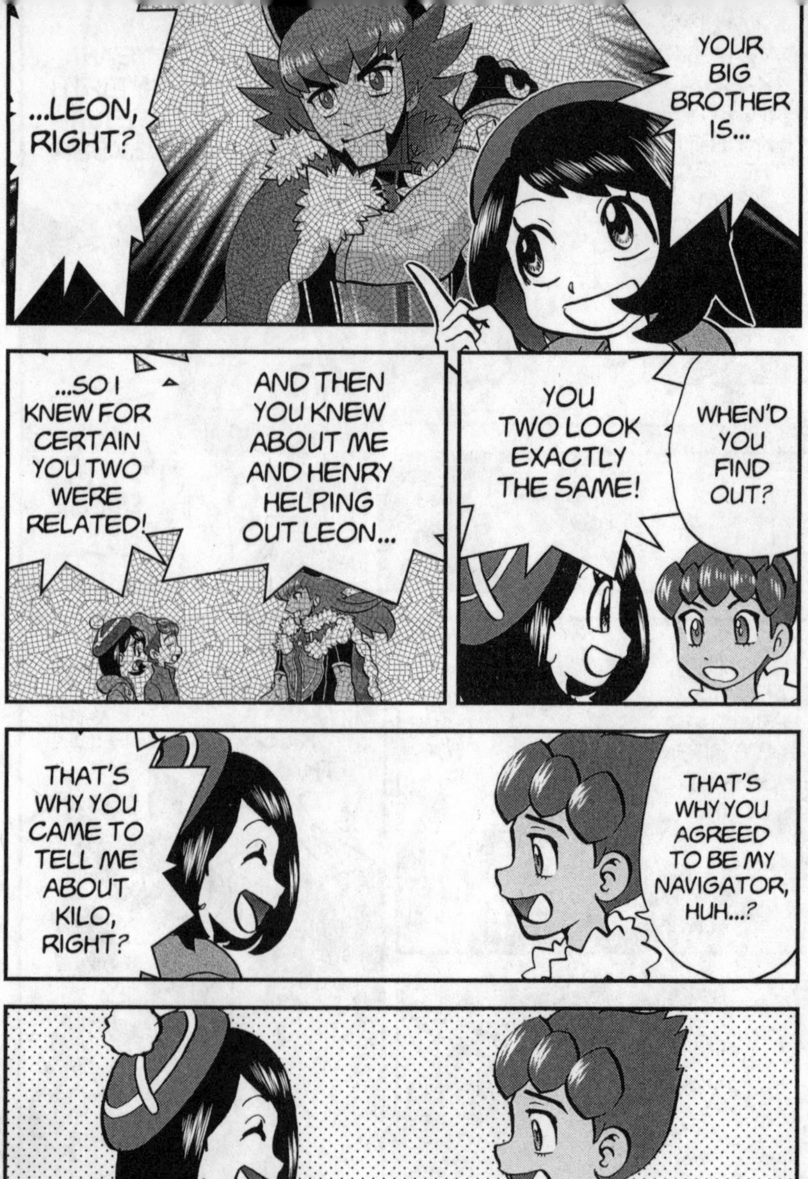
YOUR BIG BROTHER IS...
...LEON, RIGHT?
WHEN'D YOU FIND OUT?
YOU TWO LOOK EXACTLY THE SAME!
AND THEN YOU KNEW ABOUT ME AND HENRY HELPING OUT LEON...
...SO I KNEW FOR CERTAIN YOU TWO WERE RELATED!
THAT'S WHY YOU AGREED TO BE MY NAVIGATOR, HUH...?
THAT'S WHY YOU CAME TO TELL ME ABOUT KILO, RIGHT?

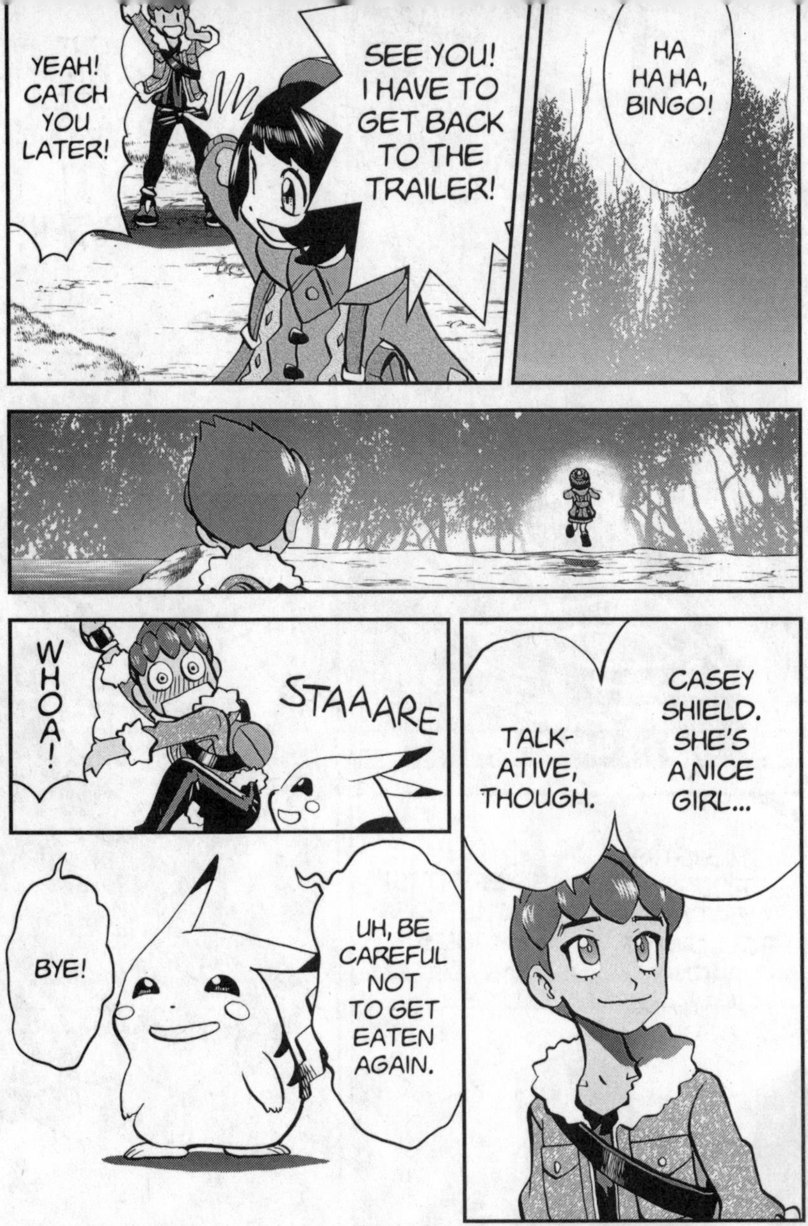
HA HA HA, BINGO!
SEE YOU! I HAVE TO GET BACK TO THE TRAILER!
YEAH! CATCH YOU LATER!
CASEY SHIELD. SHE'S A NICE GIRL...
TALK-ATIVE, THOUGH.
STAAARE
WHOA!
UH, BE CAREFUL NOT TO GET EATEN AGAIN.
BYE!

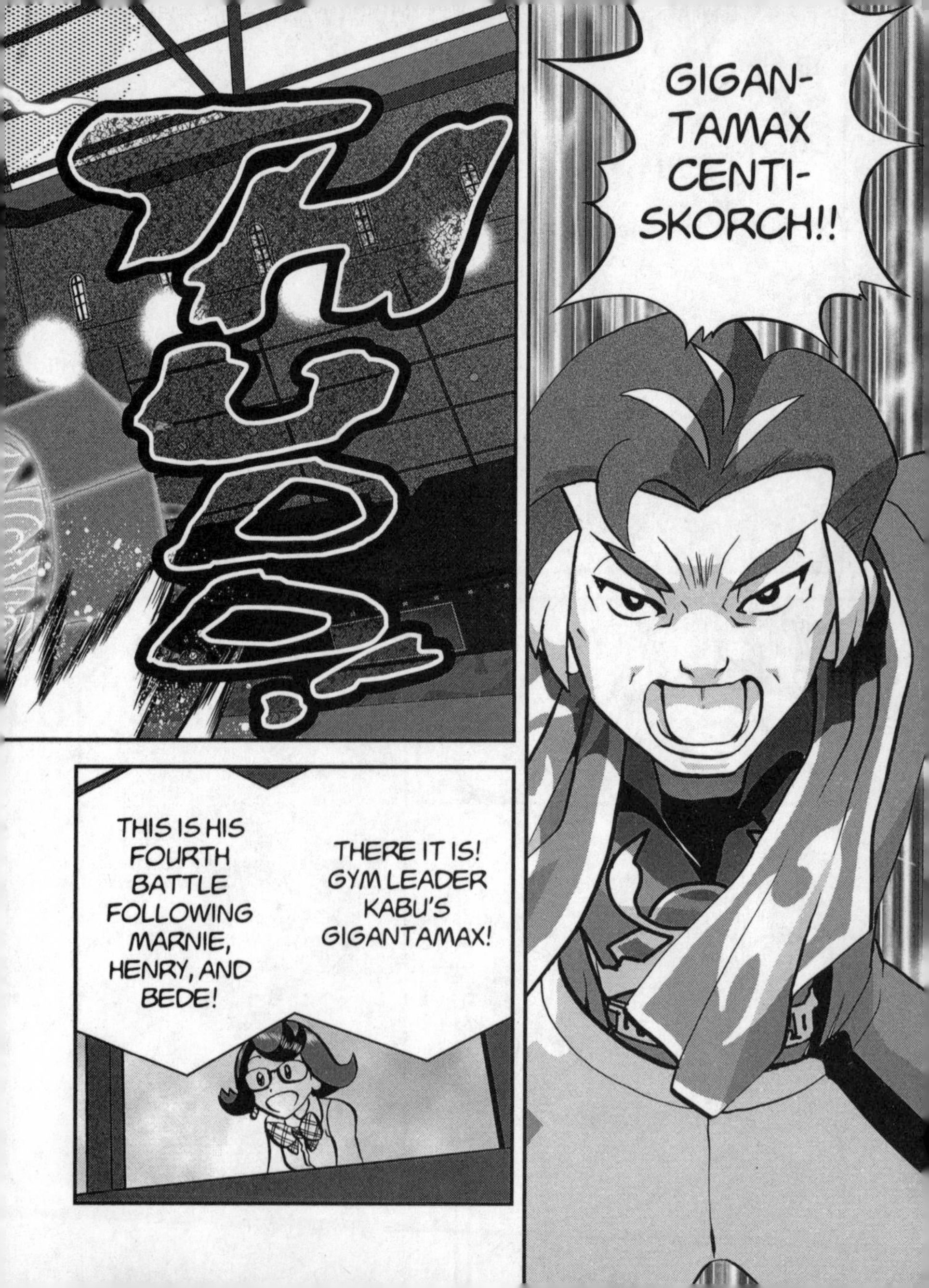
GIGANTAMAX CENTISKORCH!!
THERE IT IS! GYM LEADER KABU'S GIGANTAMAX!
THIS IS HIS FOURTH BATTLE FOLLOWING MARNIE, HENRY, AND BEDE!

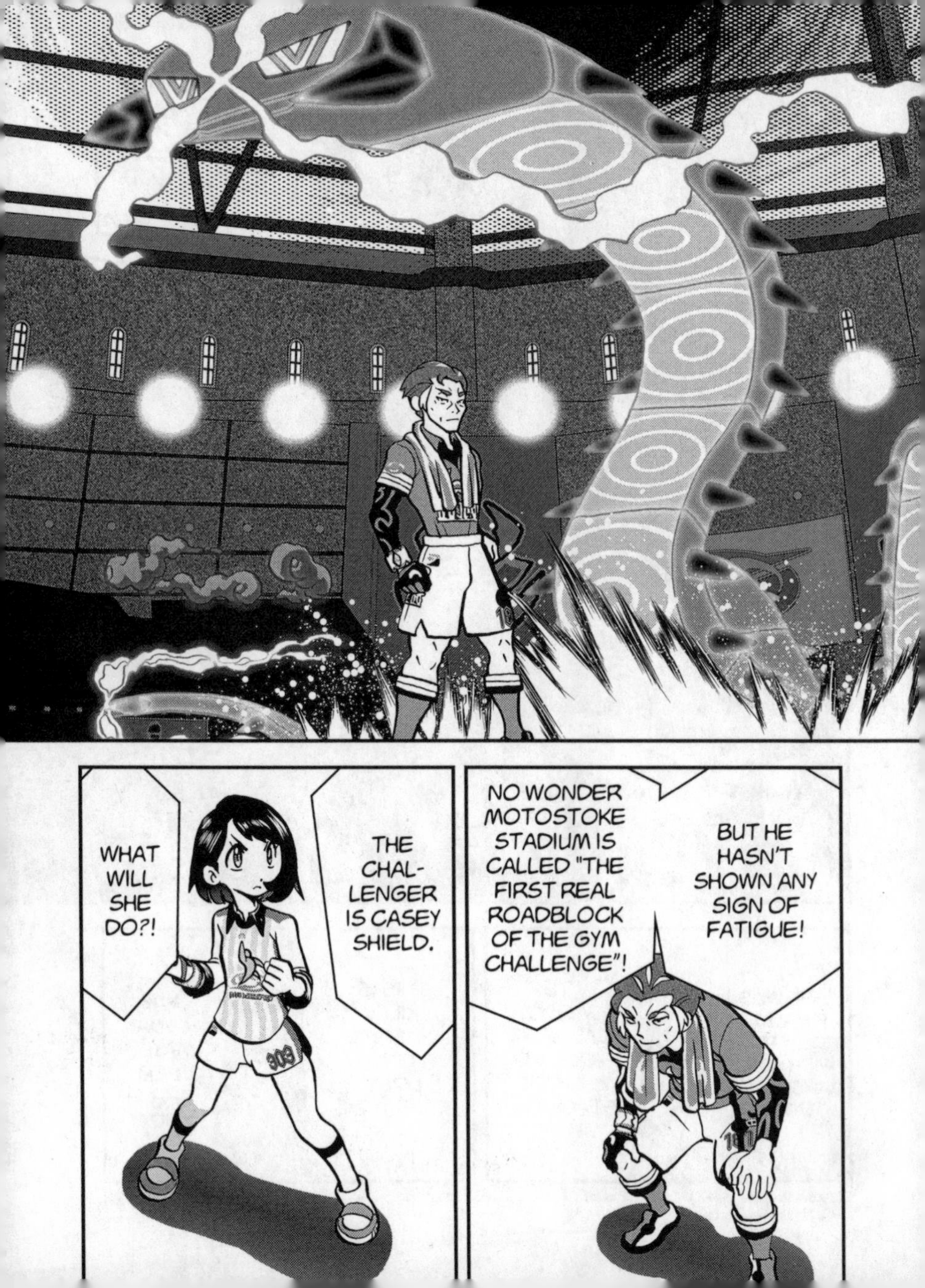
NO WONDER MOTOSTOKE STADIUM IS CALLED "THE FIRST REAL ROADBLOCK OF THE GYM CHALLENGE"!
BUT HE HASN'T SHOWN ANY SIGN OF FATIGUE!
THE CHAL-LENGER IS CASEY SHIELD.
WHAT WILL SHE DO?!

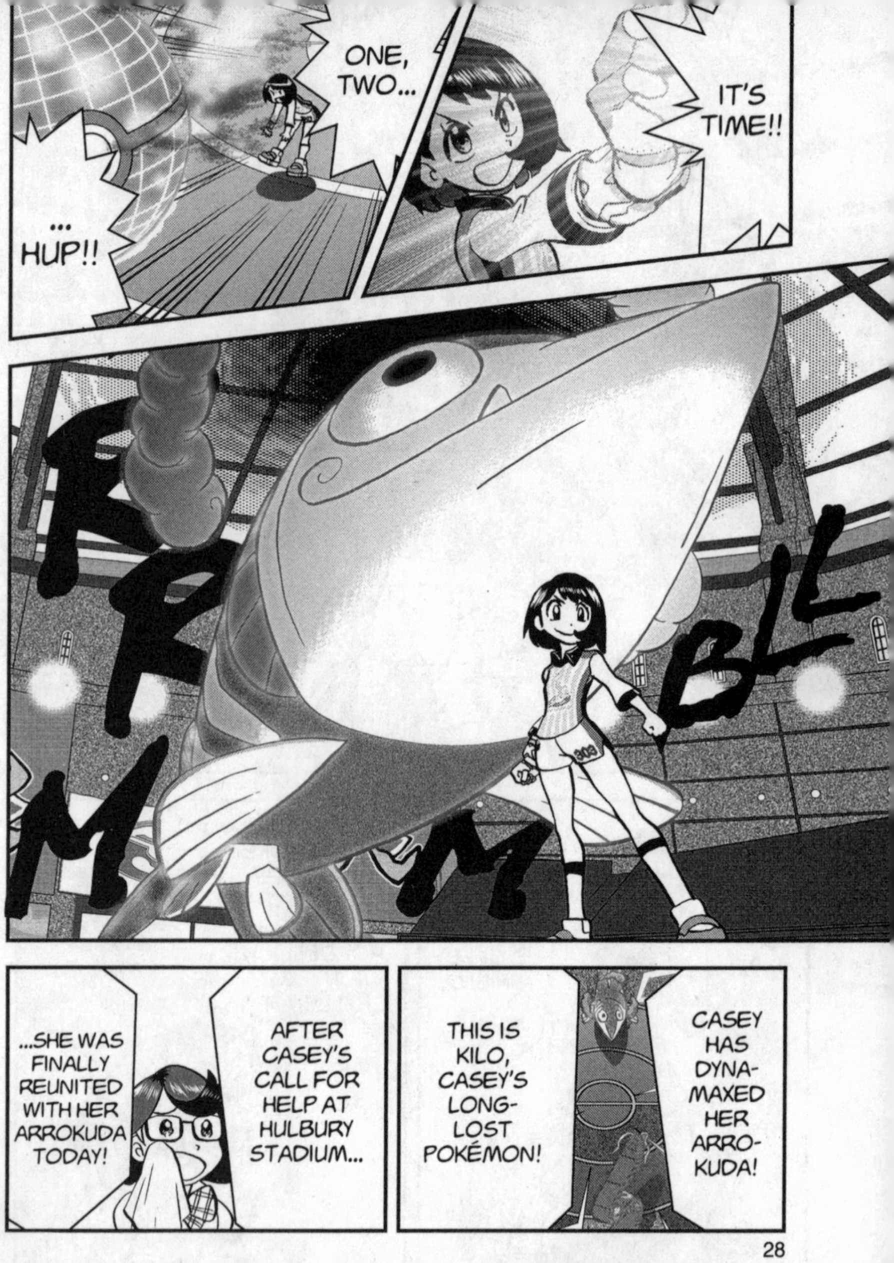
IT'S TIME!!
ONE, TWO...
...HUP!!
RRMMBLE
CASEY HAS DYNA-MAXED HER ARRO-KUDA!
THIS IS KILO, CASEY'S LONG-LOST POKÉMON!
AFTER CASEY'S CALL FOR HELP AT HULBURY STADIUM...
...SHE WAS FINALLY REUNITED WITH HER ARROKUDA TODAY!

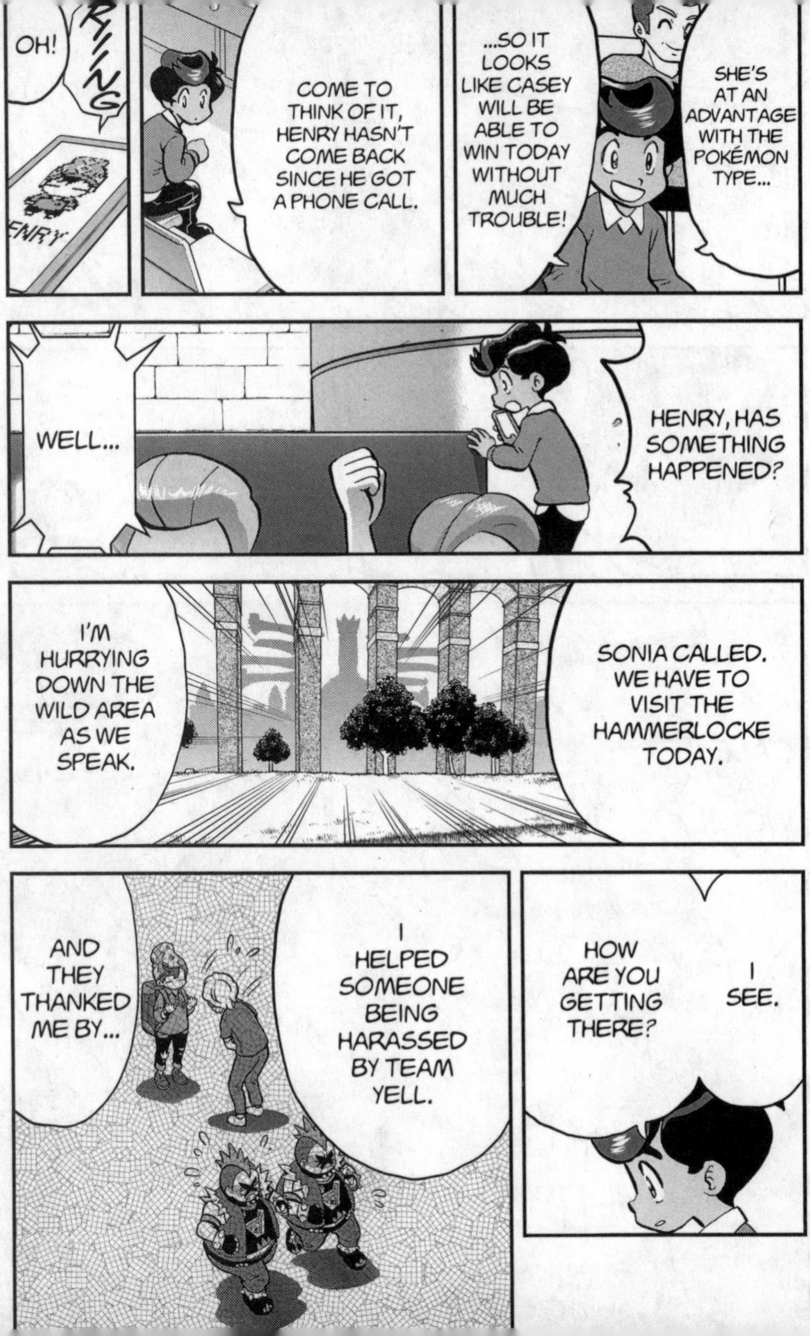
SHE'S AT AN ADVANTAGE WITH THE POKéMON TYPE...
...SO IT LOOKS LIKE CASEY WILL BE ABLE TO WIN TODAY WITHOUT MUCH TROUBLE!
COME TO THINK OF IT, HENRY HASN'T COME BACK SINCE HE GOT A PHONE CALL.
RIIING
OH!
HENRY
HENRY, HAS SOMETHING HAPPENED?
WELL...
SONIA CALLED. WE HAVE TO VISIT THE HAMMERLOCKE TODAY.
I'M HURRYING DOWN THE WILD AREA AS WE SPEAK.
I SEE.
HOW ARE YOU GETTING THERE?
I HELPED SOMEONE BEING HARASSED BY TEAM YELL.
AND THEY THANKED ME BY...

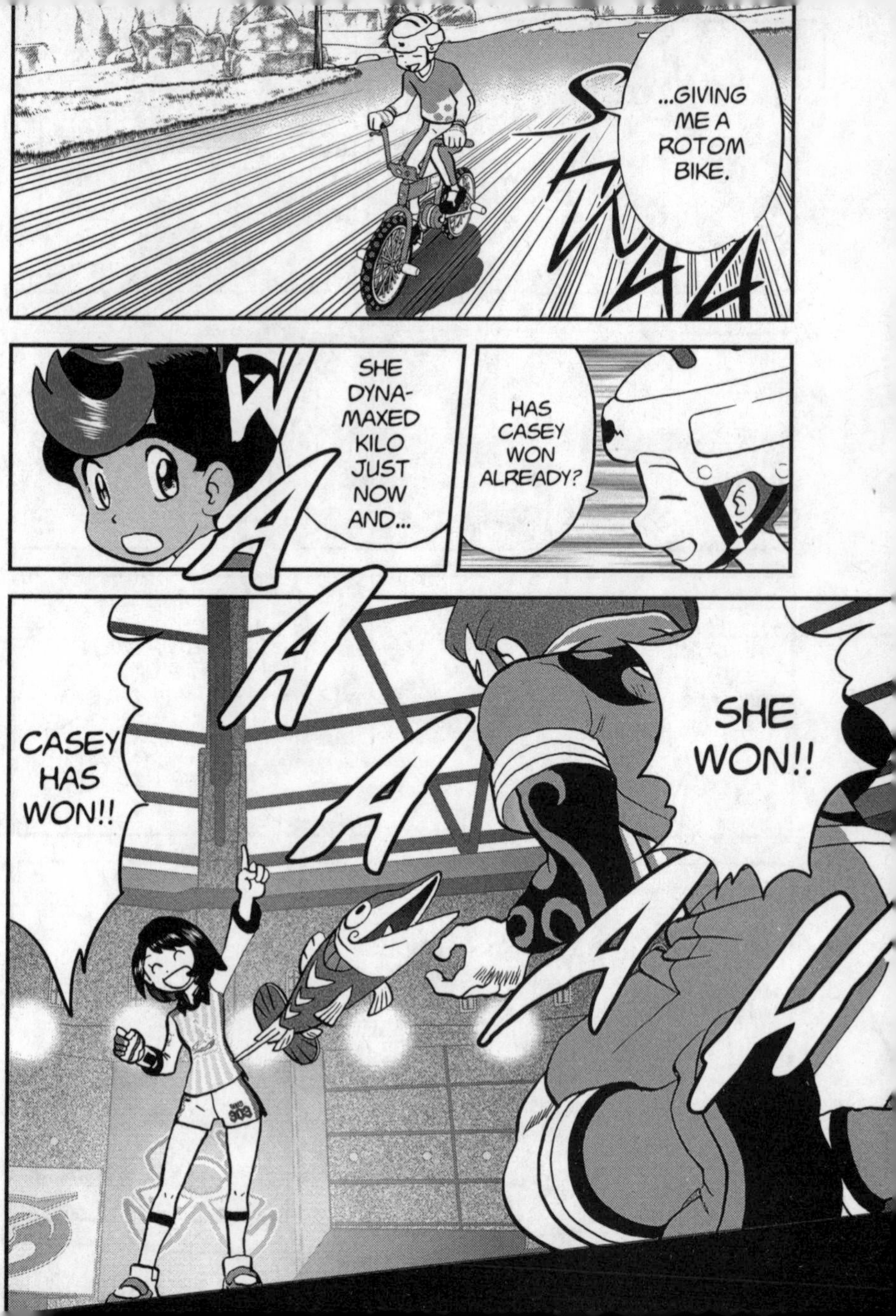
...GIVING ME A ROTOM BIKE.
HAS CASEY WON ALREADY?
SHE DYNA-MAXED KILO JUST NOW AND...
WAAAAAH
SHE WON!!
CASEY HAS WON!!

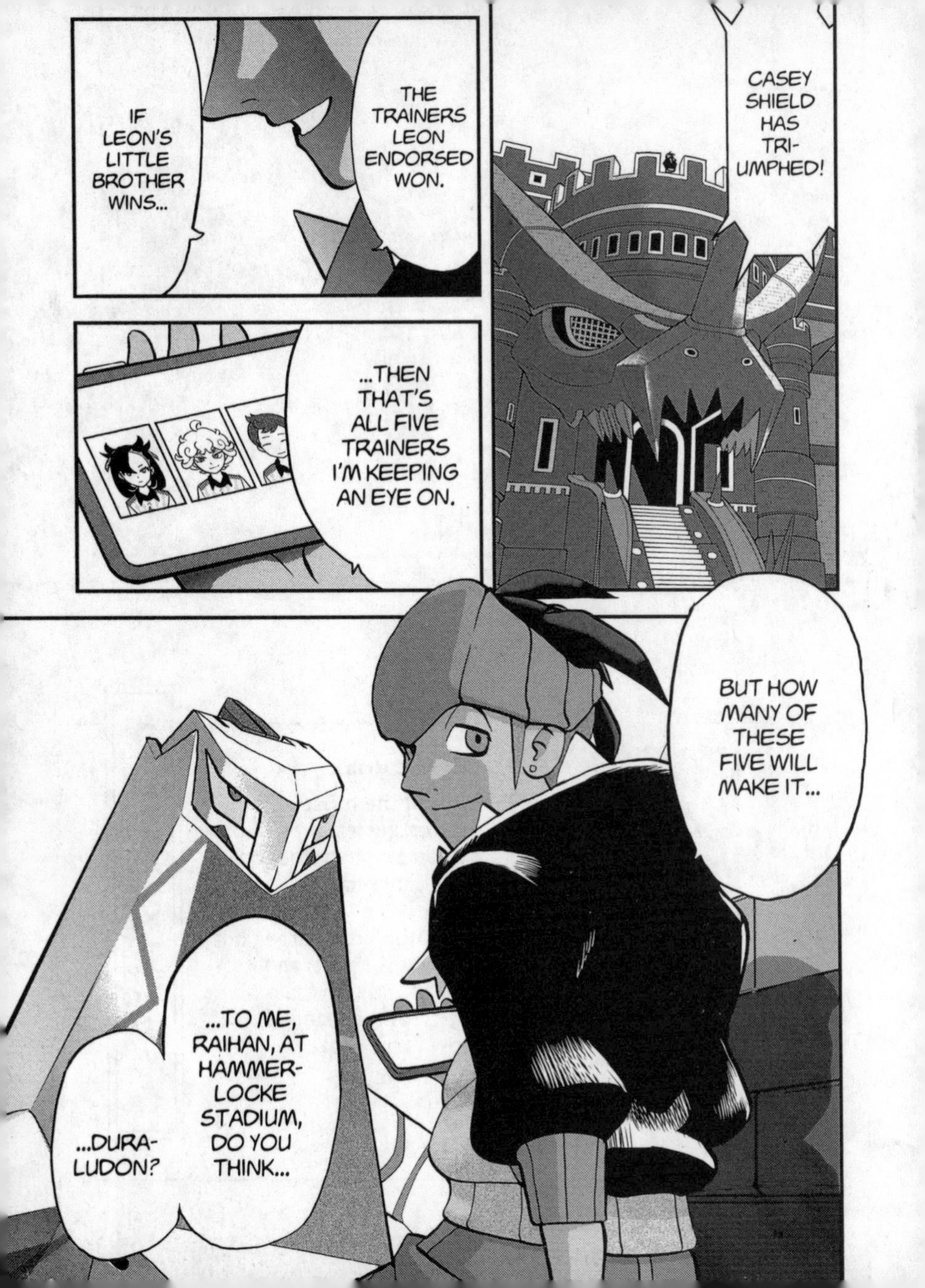
CASEY SHIELD HAS TRI- UMPHED!
THE TRAINERS LEON ENDORSED WON.
IF LEON'S LITTLE BROTHER WINS...
...THEN THAT'S ALL FIVE TRAINERS I'M KEEPING AN EYE ON.
BUT HOW MANY OF THESE FIVE WILL MAKE IT...
...TO ME, RAIHAN, AT HAMMER- LOCKE STADIUM, DO YOU THINK...
...DURA- LUDON?

THE SECRETS OF DYNAMAX, PART 10

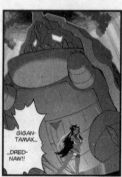

GIGAN-TAMAX...
...DRED-NAW!!

▲ When Nessa's Drednaw Gigantamaxed, it stood 78'09" tall.

Gigantamax

One of the most interesting features of the Dynamax phenomenon is "Gigantamaxing." Not only does a Gigantimaxed Pokémon grow larger, but it changes shape, and its power and moves are greatly enhanced. How terrifying!

Adventure 12 Thump!! The Gazing Sage

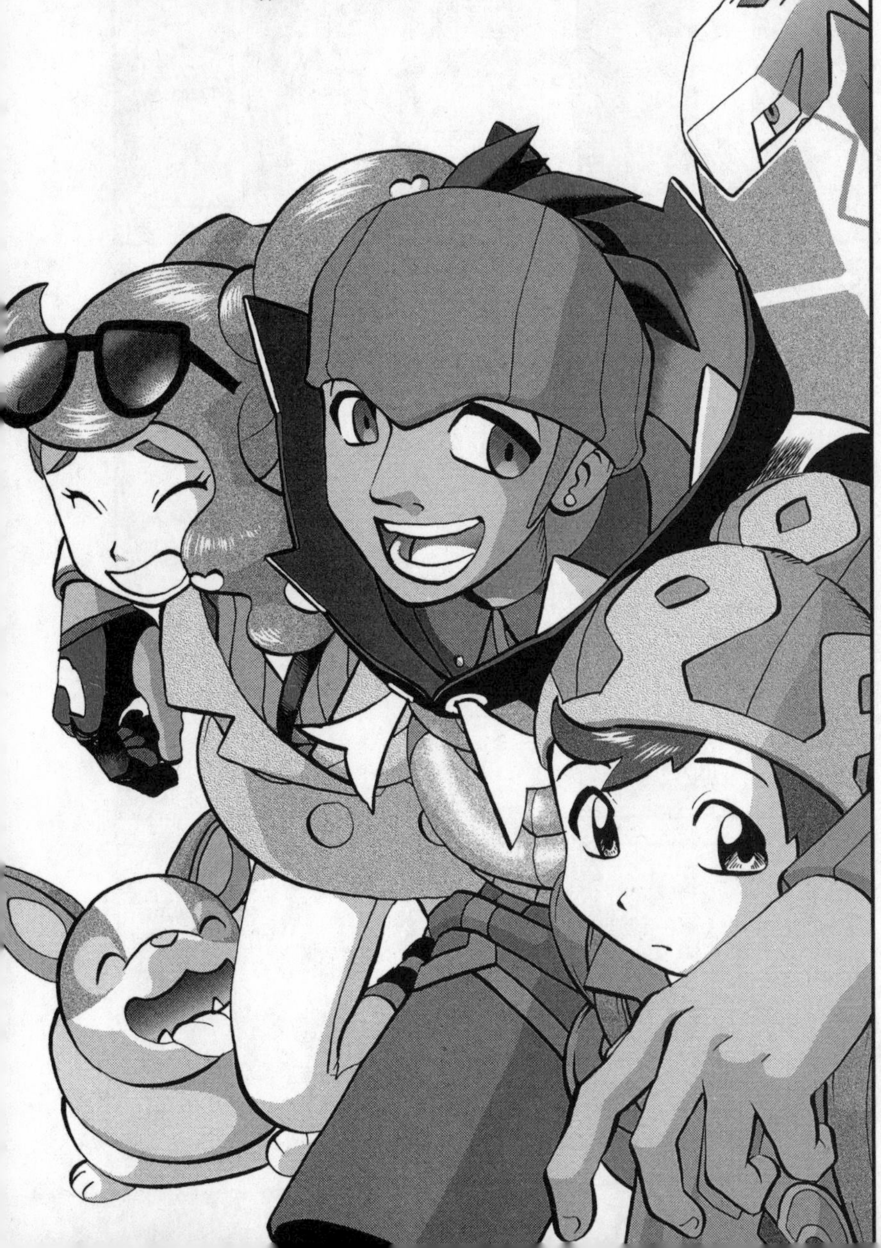

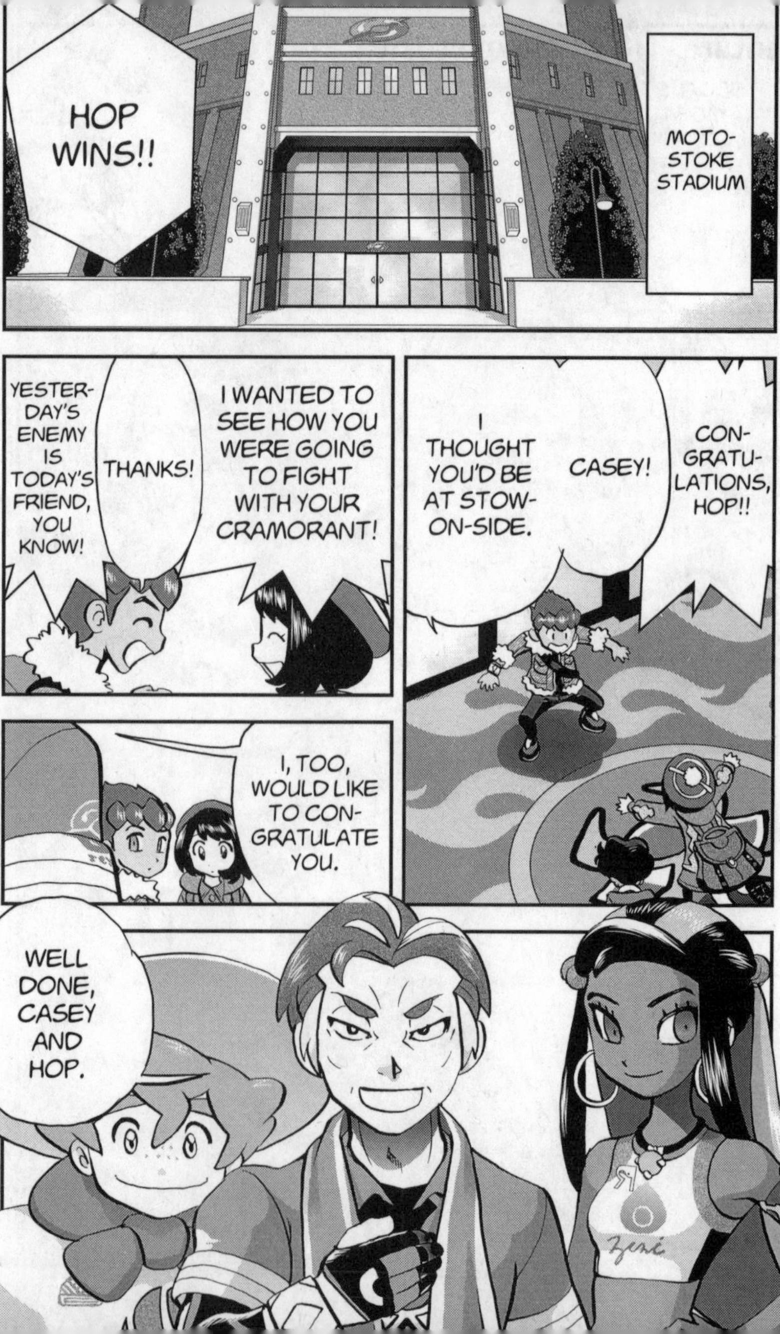
MOTO-STOKE STADIUM
HOP WINS!!
CON-GRATU-LATIONS, HOP!!
CASEY!
I THOUGHT YOU'D BE AT STOW-ON-SIDE.
I WANTED TO SEE HOW YOU WERE GOING TO FIGHT WITH YOUR CRAMORANT!
THANKS!
YESTER-DAY'S ENEMY IS TODAY'S FRIEND, YOU KNOW!
I, TOO, WOULD LIKE TO CON-GRATULATE YOU.
WELL DONE, CASEY AND HOP.

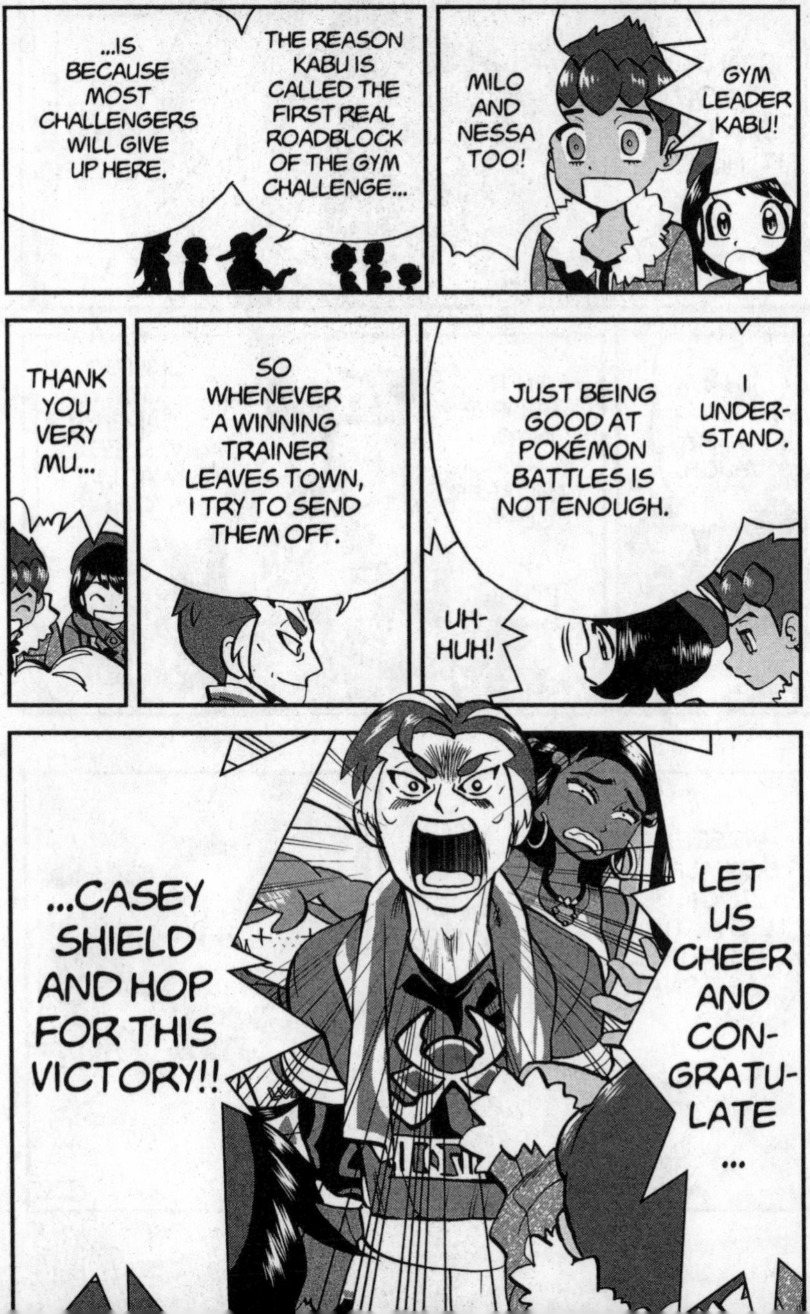
GYM LEADER KABU!
MILO AND NESSA TOO!
THE REASON KABU IS CALLED THE FIRST REAL ROADBLOCK OF THE GYM CHALLENGE...
...IS BECAUSE MOST CHALLENGERS WILL GIVE UP HERE.
I UNDER-STAND.
JUST BEING GOOD AT POKÉMON BATTLES IS NOT ENOUGH.
UH-HUH!
SO WHENEVER A WINNING TRAINER LEAVES TOWN, I TRY TO SEND THEM OFF.
THANK YOU VERY MU...
LET US CHEER AND CON-GRATU-LATE...
...CASEY SHIELD AND HOP FOR THIS VICTORY!!

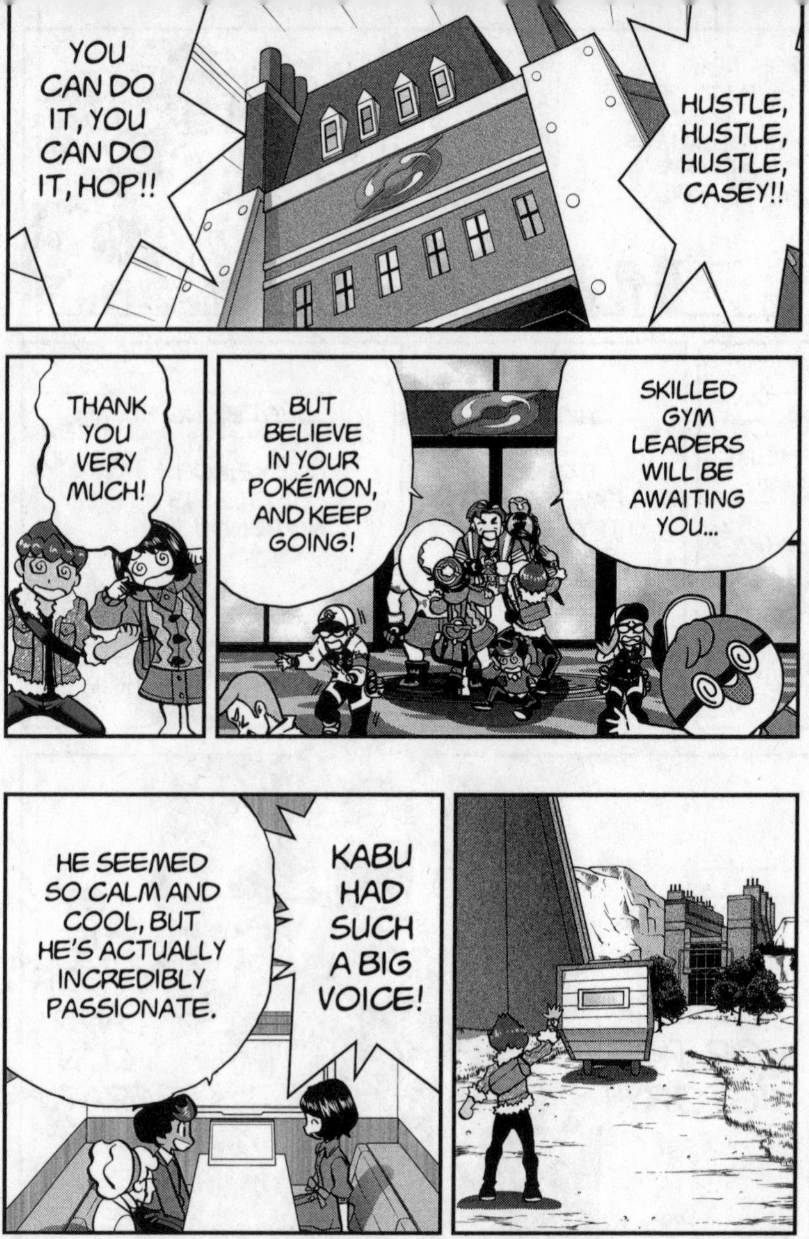
HUSTLE, HUSTLE, HUSTLE, CASEY!!
YOU CAN DO IT, YOU CAN DO IT, HOP!!
SKILLED GYM LEADERS WILL BE AWAITING YOU...
BUT BELIEVE IN YOUR POKÉMON, AND KEEP GOING!
THANK YOU VERY MUCH!
KABU HAD SUCH A BIG VOICE!
HE SEEMED SO CALM AND COOL, BUT HE'S ACTUALLY INCREDIBLY PASSIONATE.

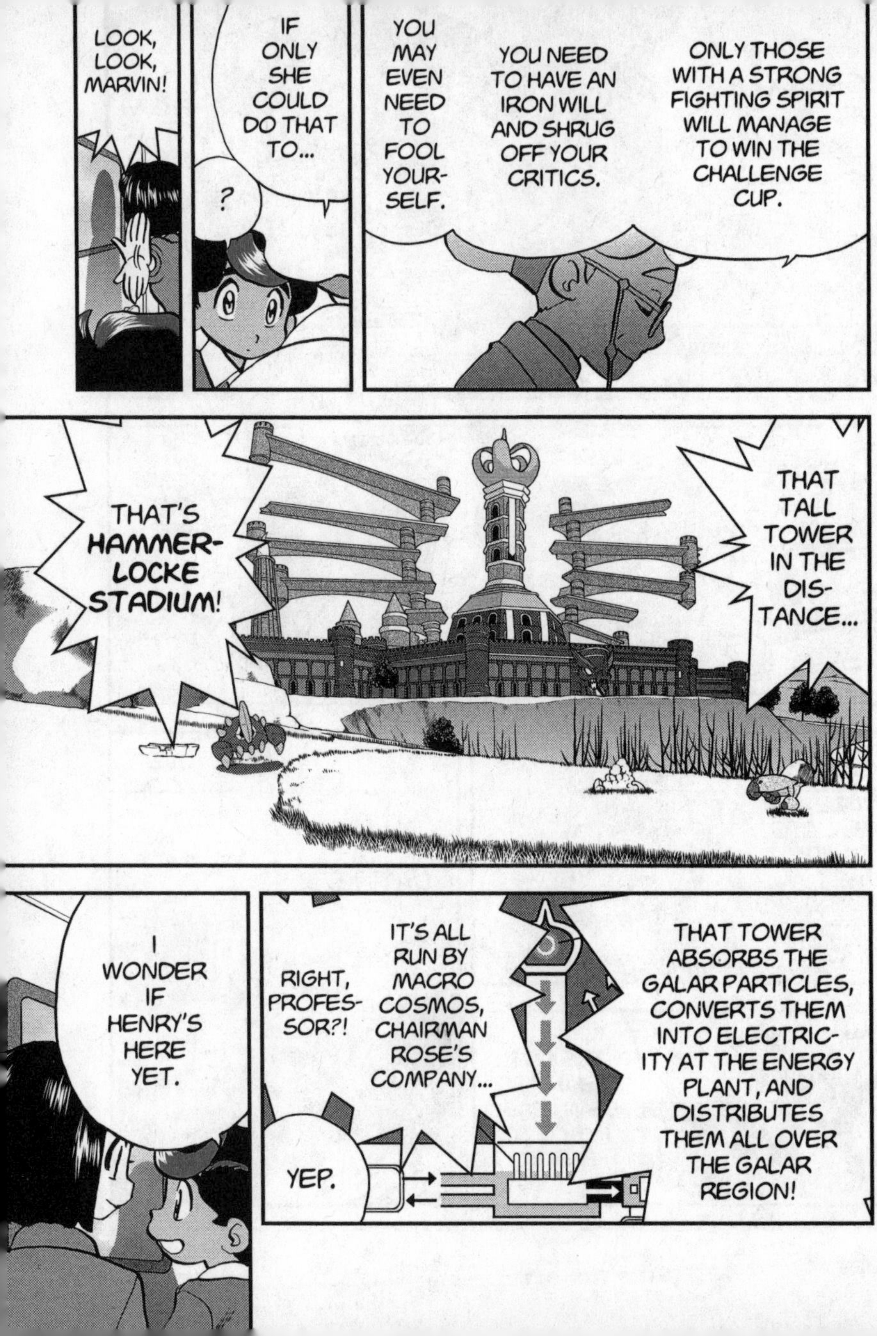
ONLY THOSE WITH A STRONG FIGHTING SPIRIT WILL MANAGE TO WIN THE CHALLENGE CUP.
YOU NEED TO HAVE AN IRON WILL AND SHRUG OFF YOUR CRITICS.
YOU MAY EVEN NEED TO FOOL YOUR-SELF.
IF ONLY SHE COULD DO THAT TO...
?
LOOK, LOOK, MARVIN!
THAT TALL TOWER IN THE DIS-TANCE...
THAT'S HAMMER-LOCKE STADIUM!
THAT TOWER ABSORBS THE GALAR PARTICLES, CONVERTS THEM INTO ELECTRIC-ITY AT THE ENERGY PLANT, AND DISTRIBUTES THEM ALL OVER THE GALAR REGION!
IT'S ALL RUN BY MACRO COSMOS, CHAIRMAN ROSE'S COMPANY...
RIGHT, PROFES-SOR?!
YEP.
I WONDER IF HENRY'S HERE YET.

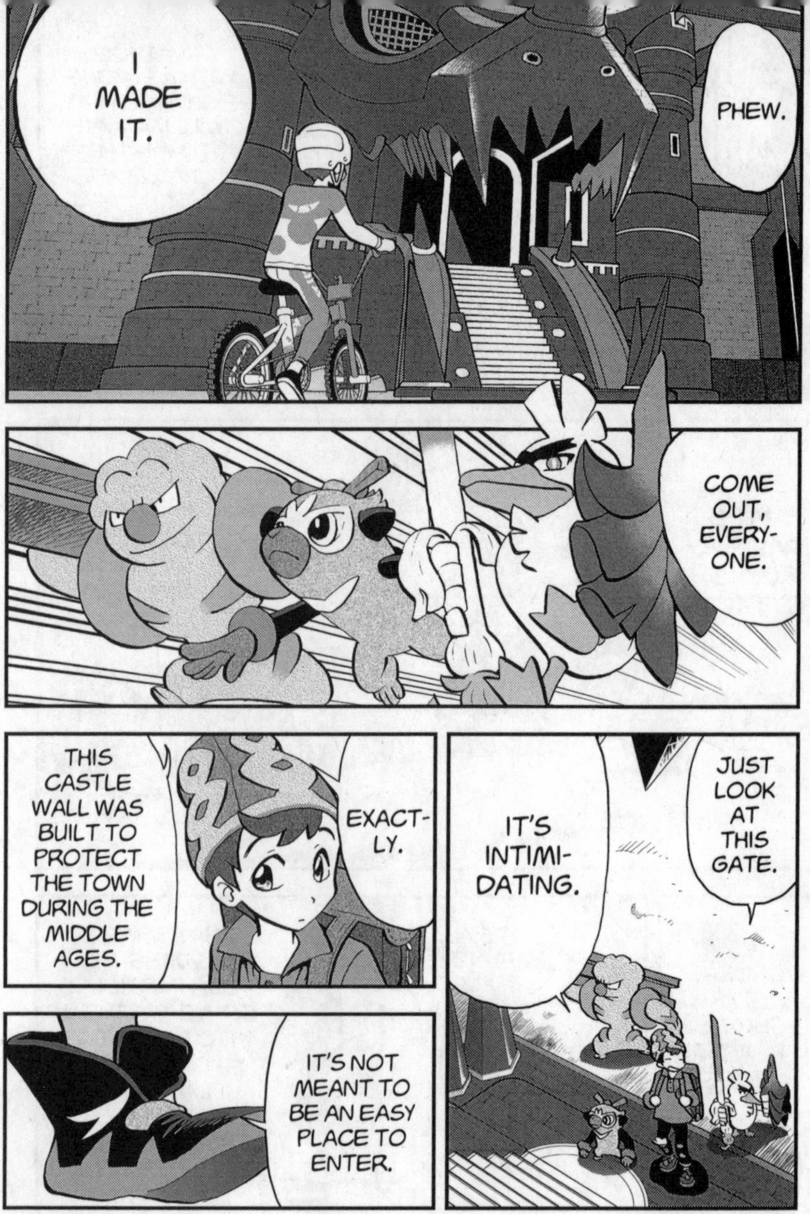
PHEW.
I MADE IT.
COME OUT, EVERY-ONE.
JUST LOOK AT THIS GATE.
IT'S INTIMI-DATING.
EXACT-LY.
THIS CASTLE WALL WAS BUILT TO PROTECT THE TOWN DURING THE MIDDLE AGES.
IT'S NOT MEANT TO BE AN EASY PLACE TO ENTER.

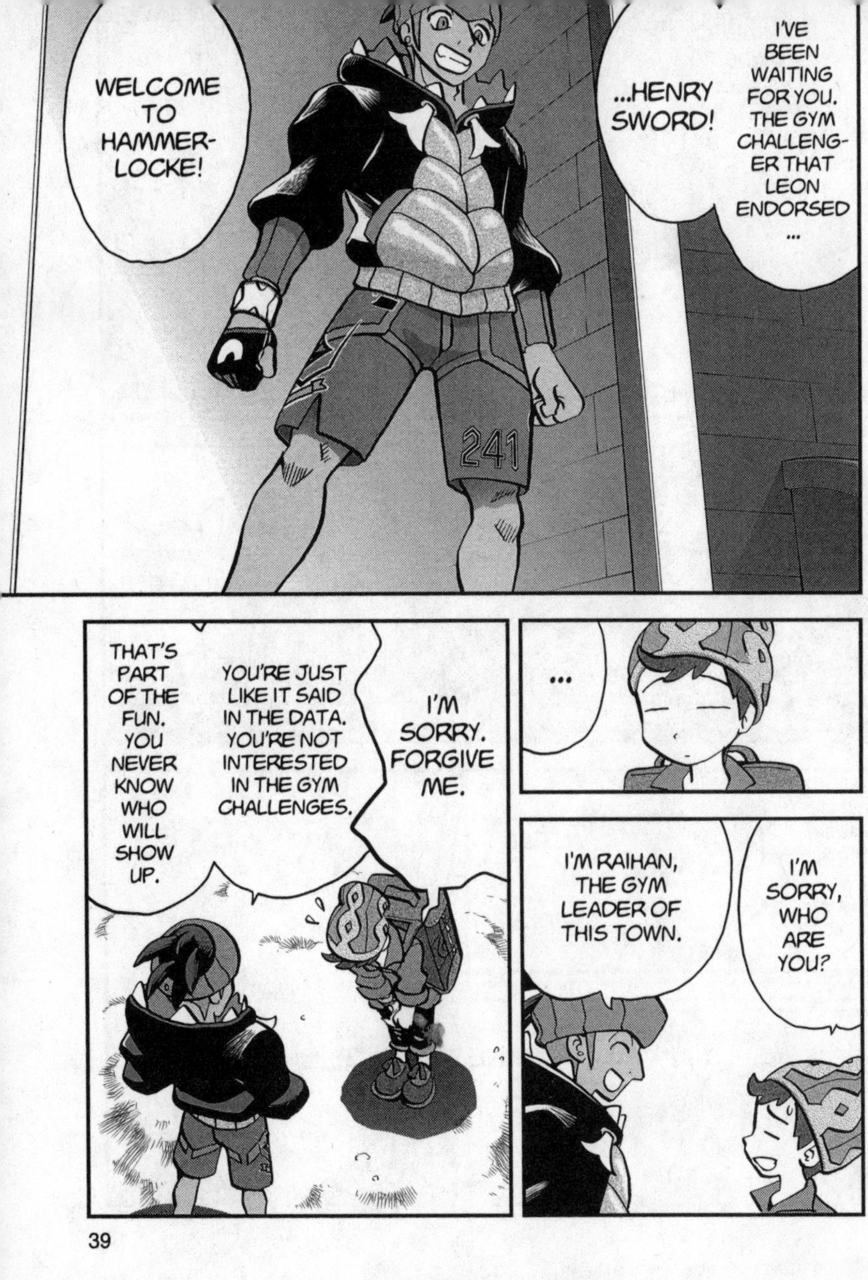

I'VE BEEN WAITING FOR YOU. THE GYM CHALLENGER THAT LEON ENDORSED ...
...HENRY SWORD!
WELCOME TO HAMMERLOCKE!
241
...
I'M SORRY, WHO ARE YOU?
I'M RAIHAN, THE GYM LEADER OF THIS TOWN.
I'M SORRY. FORGIVE ME.
YOU'RE JUST LIKE IT SAID IN THE DATA. YOU'RE NOT INTERESTED IN THE GYM CHALLENGES.
THAT'S PART OF THE FUN. YOU NEVER KNOW WHO WILL SHOW UP.

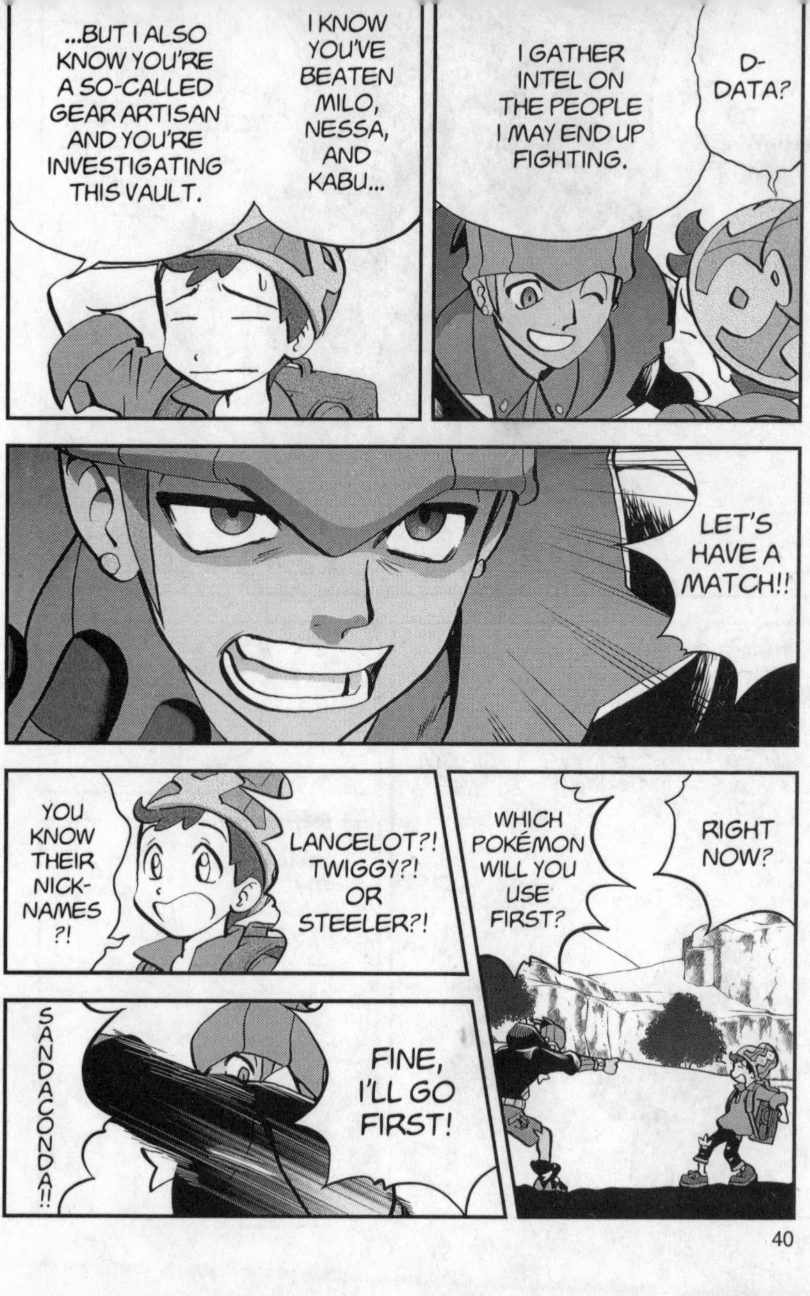
D-DATA?
I GATHER INTEL ON THE PEOPLE I MAY END UP FIGHTING.
I KNOW YOU'VE BEATEN MILO, NESSA, AND KABU...
...BUT I ALSO KNOW YOU'RE A SO-CALLED GEAR ARTISAN AND YOU'RE INVESTIGATING THIS VAULT.
LET'S HAVE A MATCH!!
RIGHT NOW?
WHICH POKÉMON WILL YOU USE FIRST?
LANCELOT?! TWIGGY?! OR STEELER?!
YOU KNOW THEIR NICK-NAMES?!
FINE, I'LL GO FIRST!
SANDACONDA!!

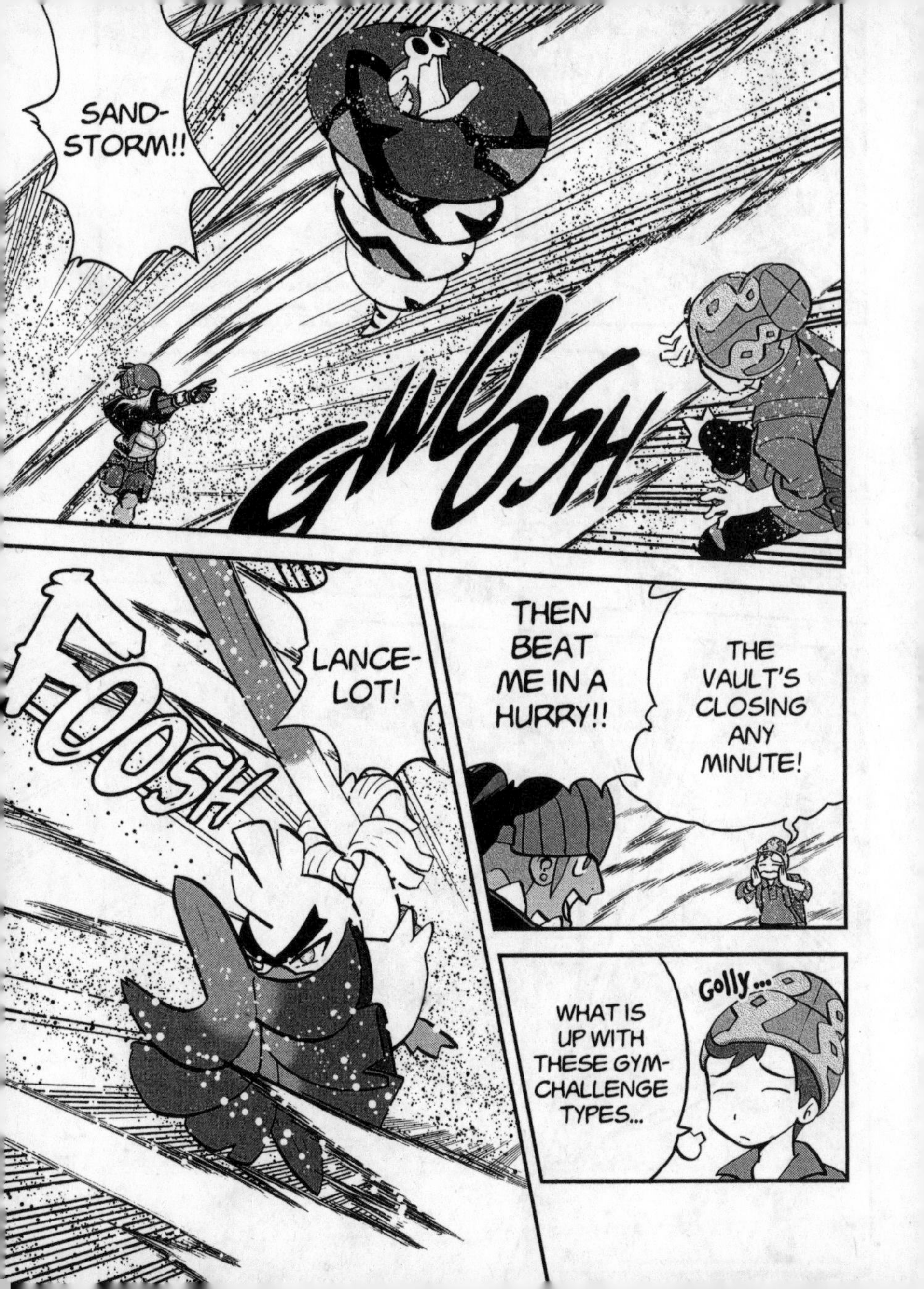
SAND-STORM!!
GWOOSH
THE VAULT'S CLOSING ANY MINUTE!
THEN BEAT ME IN A HURRY!!
Golly...
WHAT IS UP WITH THESE GYM-CHALLENGE TYPES...
LANCE-LOT!
FOOSH

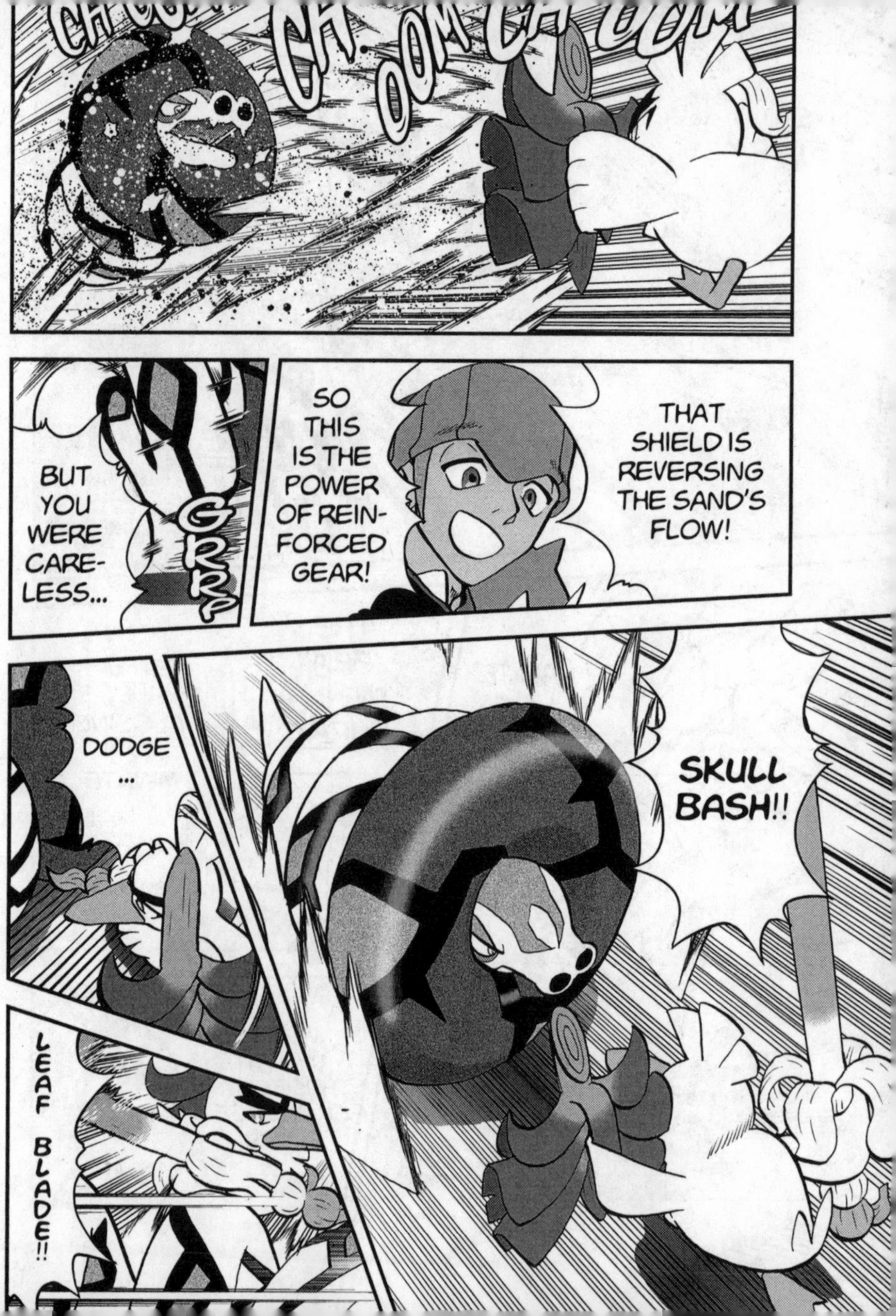

CH OOM CH OOM
THAT SHIELD IS REVERSING THE SAND'S FLOW!
SO THIS IS THE POWER OF REIN-FORCED GEAR!
GRRR
BUT YOU WERE CARE-LESS...
SKULL BASH!!
DODGE ...
LEAF BLADE!!

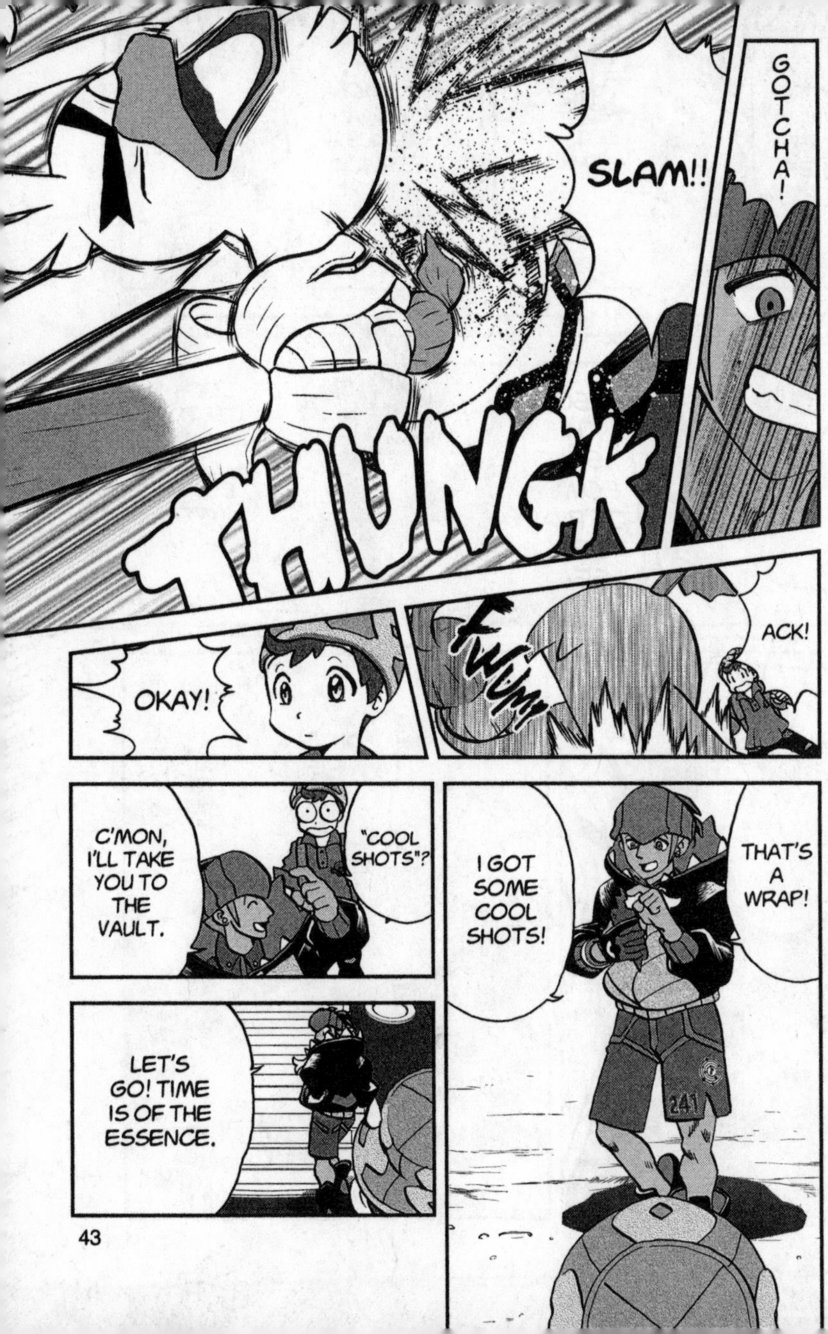
GOTCHA!
SLAM!!
THUNCK
ACK!
FWUMP
OKAY!
THAT'S A WRAP!
I GOT SOME COOL SHOTS!
"COOL SHOTS"?
C'MON, I'LL TAKE YOU TO THE VAULT.
LET'S GO! TIME IS OF THE ESSENCE.
241

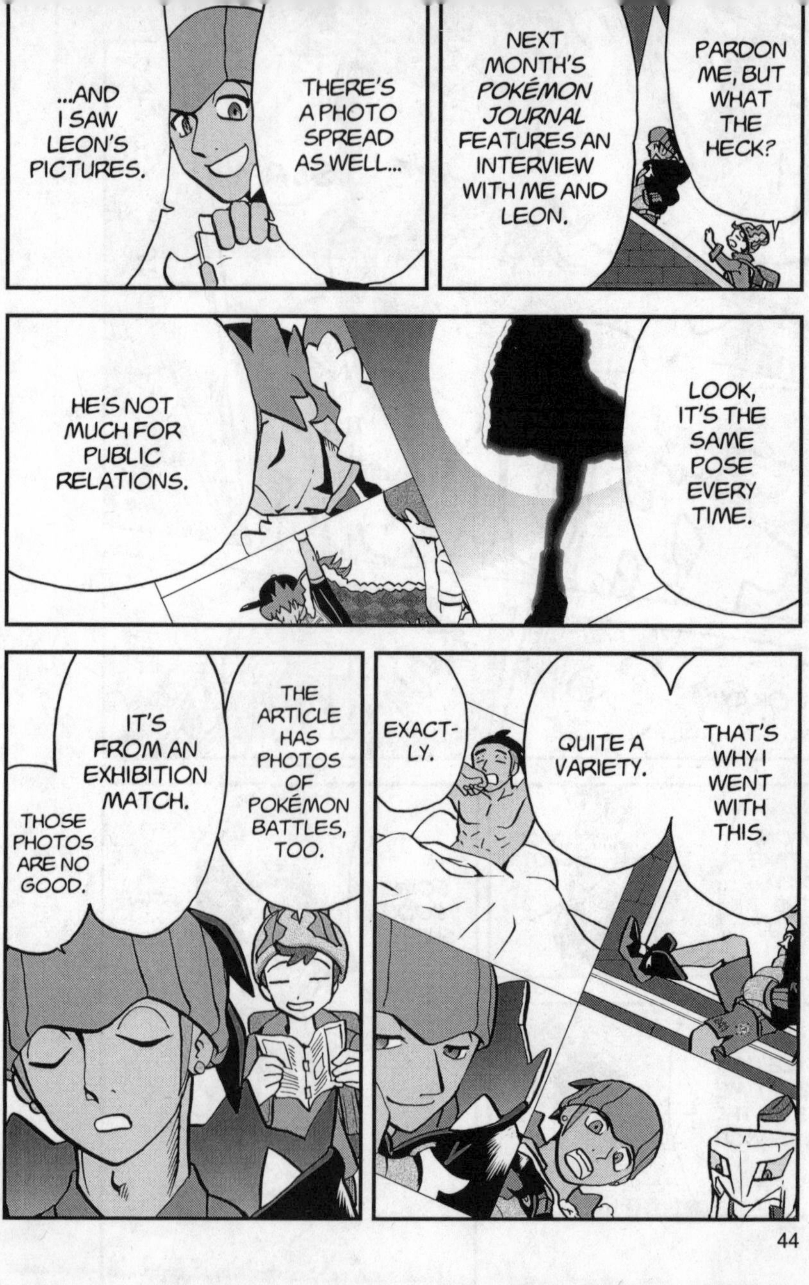
PARDON ME, BUT WHAT THE HECK?
NEXT MONTH'S POKéMON JOURNAL FEATURES AN INTERVIEW WITH ME AND LEON.
THERE'S A PHOTO SPREAD AS WELL...
...AND I SAW LEON'S PICTURES.
LOOK, IT'S THE SAME POSE EVERY TIME.
HE'S NOT MUCH FOR PUBLIC RELATIONS.
THAT'S WHY I WENT WITH THIS.
QUITE A VARIETY.
EXACT-LY.
THE ARTICLE HAS PHOTOS OF POKéMON BATTLES, TOO.
IT'S FROM AN EXHIBITION MATCH.
THOSE PHOTOS ARE NO GOOD.

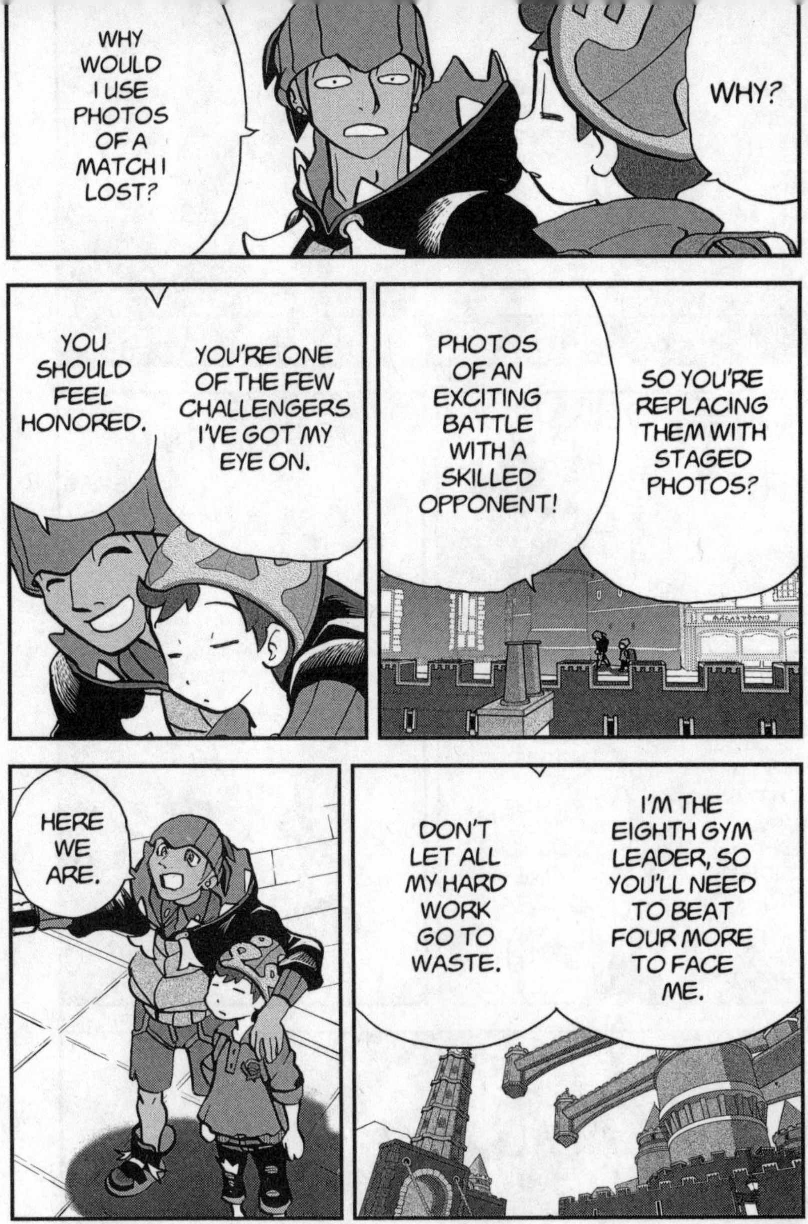
WHY?
WHY WOULD I USE PHOTOS OF A MATCH I LOST?
SO YOU'RE REPLACING THEM WITH STAGED PHOTOS?
PHOTOS OF AN EXCITING BATTLE WITH A SKILLED OPPONENT!
YOU'RE ONE OF THE FEW CHALLENGERS I'VE GOT MY EYE ON.
YOU SHOULD FEEL HONORED.
I'M THE EIGHTH GYM LEADER, SO YOU'LL NEED TO BEAT FOUR MORE TO FACE ME.
DON'T LET ALL MY HARD WORK GO TO WASTE.
HERE WE ARE.

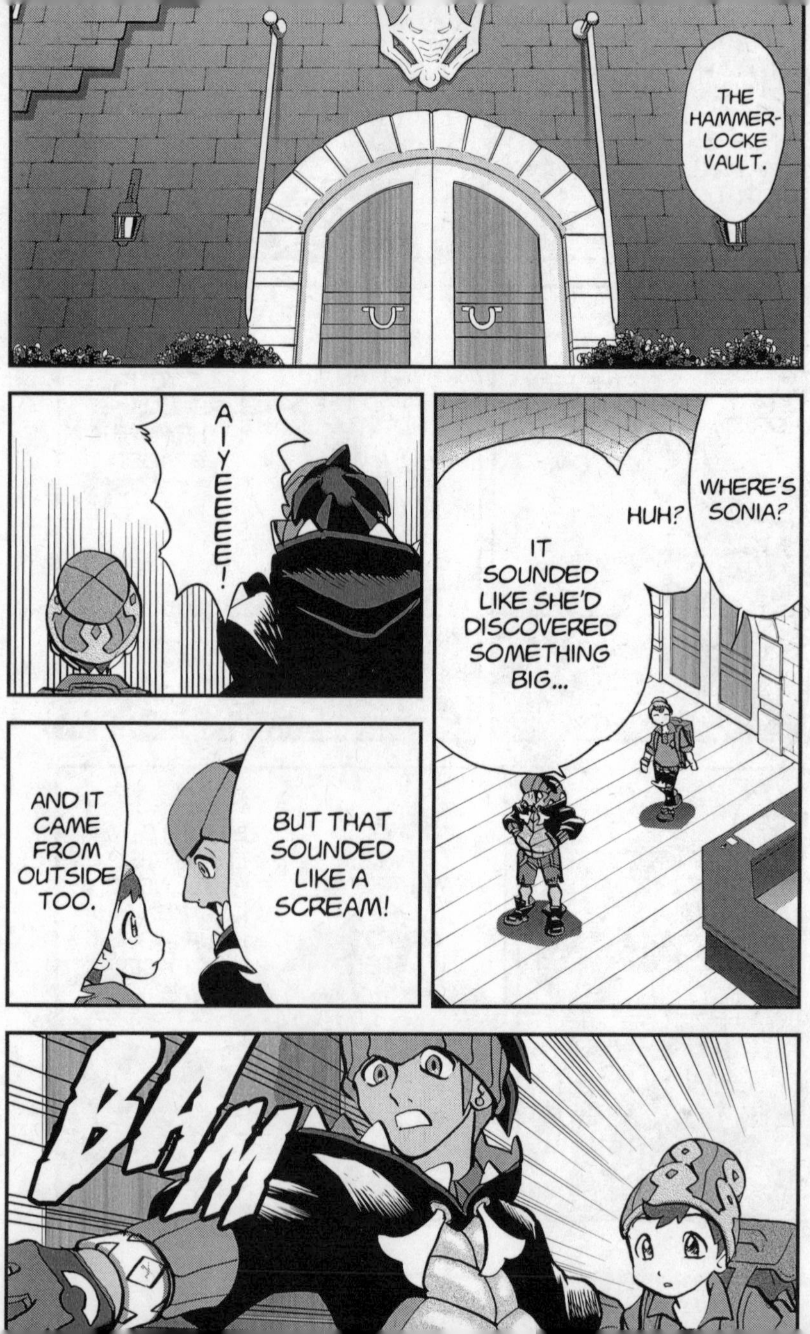
THE HAMMER-LOCKE VAULT.
WHERE'S SONIA?
HUH?
IT SOUNDED LIKE SHE'D DISCOVERED SOMETHING BIG...
AIYEEEEE!
BUT THAT SOUNDED LIKE A SCREAM!
AND IT CAME FROM OUTSIDE TOO.
BAM

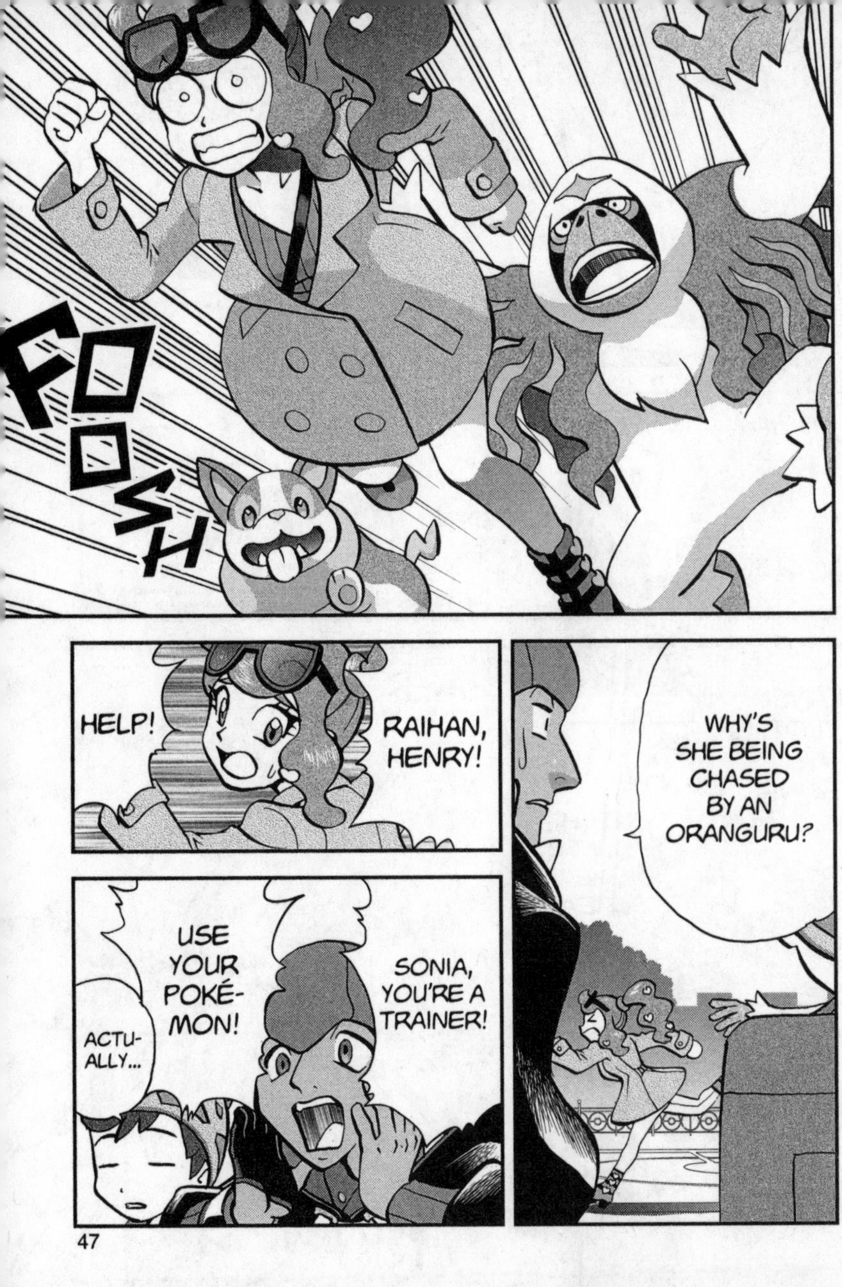
FOOSH
WHY'S SHE BEING CHASED BY AN ORANGURU?
RAIHAN, HENRY!
HELP!
SONIA, YOU'RE A TRAINER!
USE YOUR POKÉ-MON!
ACTU-ALLY...

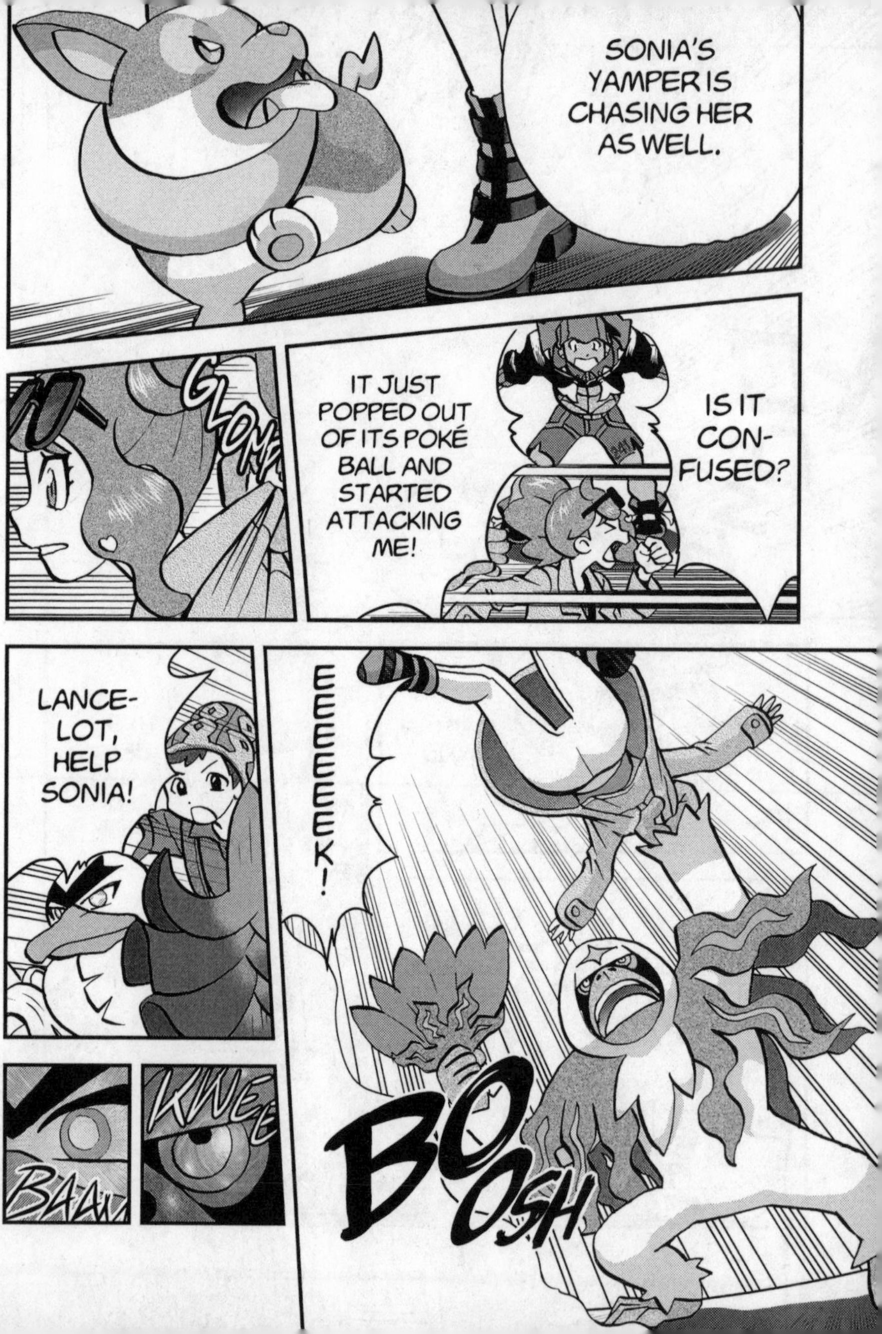
SONIA'S YAMPER IS CHASING HER AS WELL.
IS IT CON-FUSED?
IT JUST POPPED OUT OF ITS POKÉ BALL AND STARTED ATTACKING ME!
GLOMP
EEEEEEEK!
BOOSH
LANCE-LOT, HELP SONIA!
KWEE
BAAW

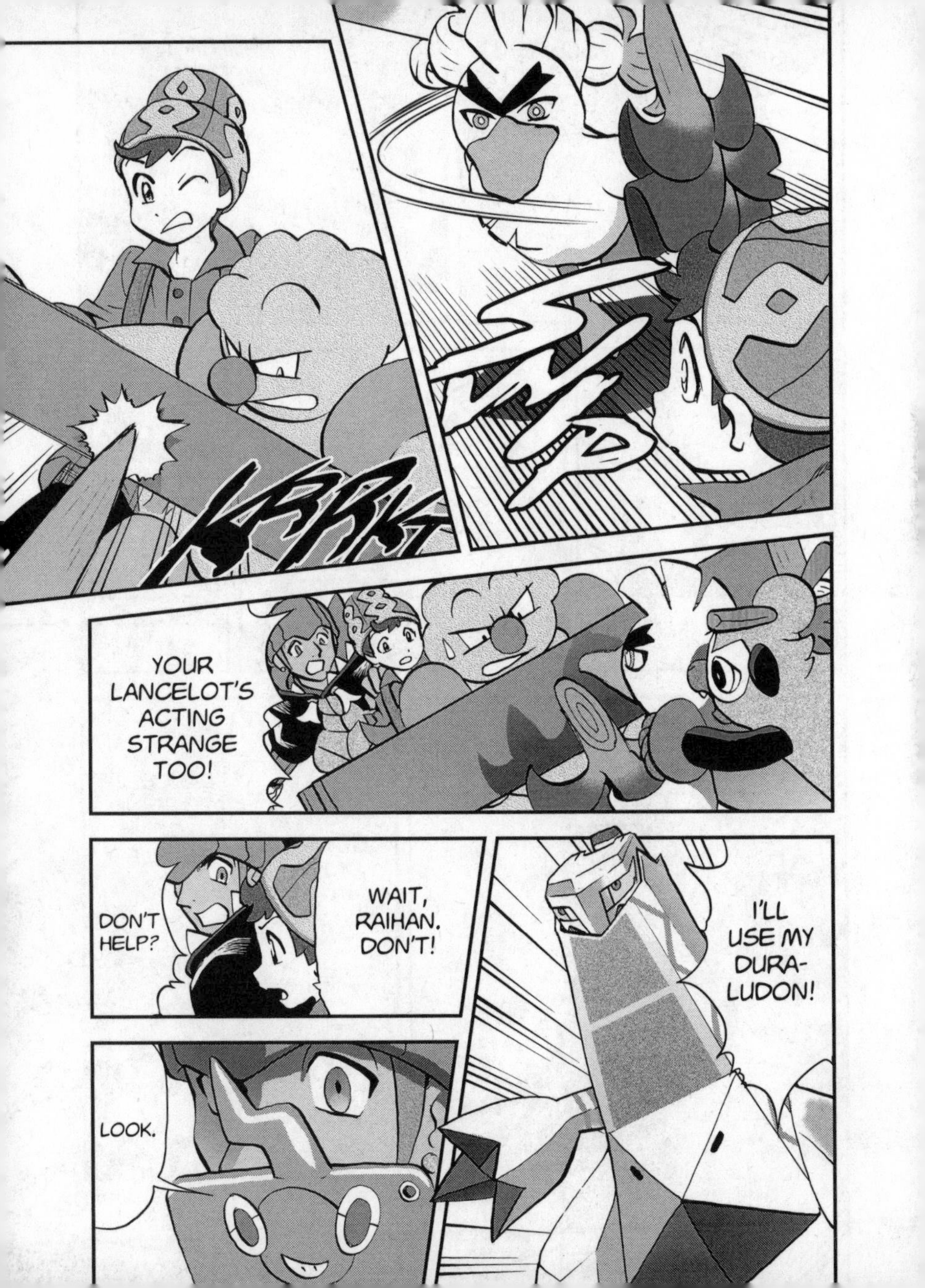
YOUR LANCELOT'S ACTING STRANGE TOO!
I'LL USE MY DURA-LUDON!
WAIT, RAIHAN. DON'T!
DON'T HELP?
LOOK.

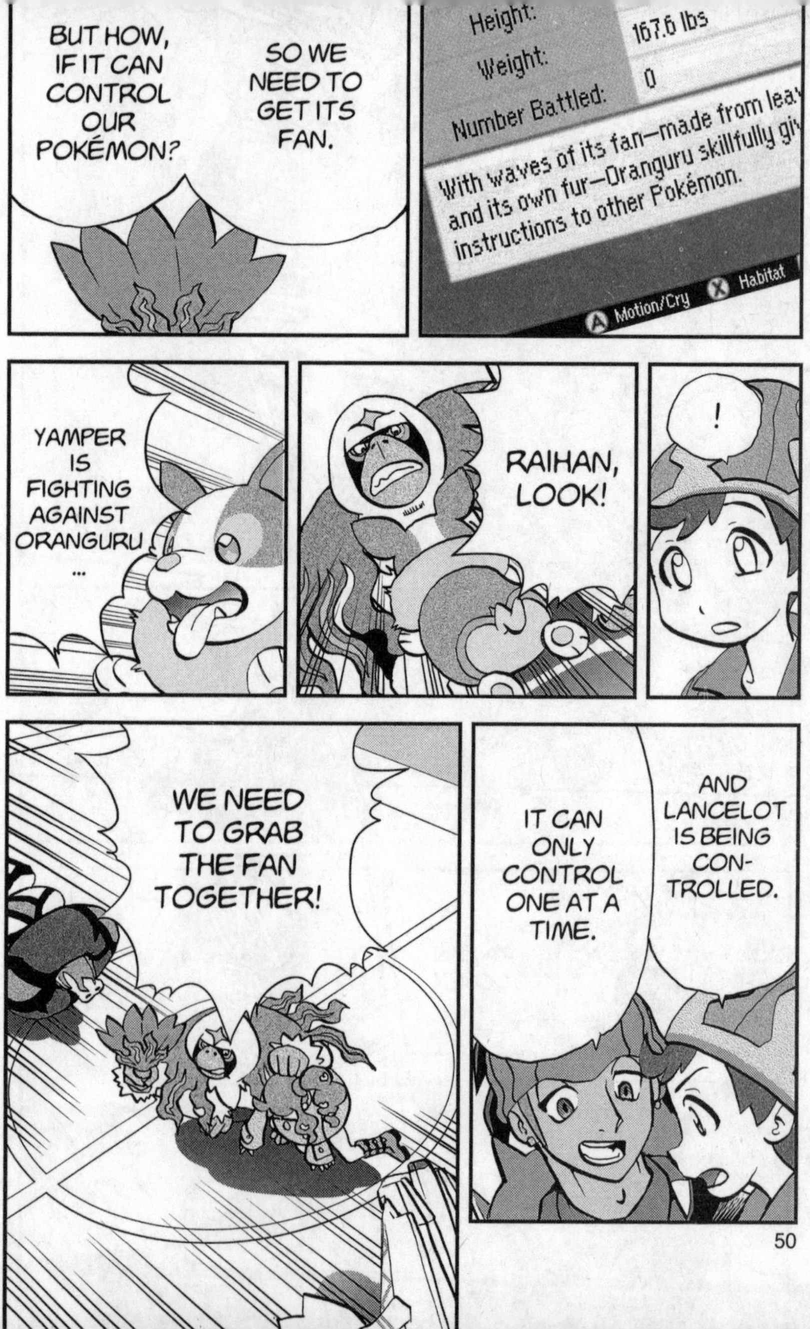
Height:
167.6 lbs
Weight:
0
Number Battled:
With waves of its fan—made from leav
and its own fur—Oranguru skillfully giv
instructions to other Pokémon.
Motion/Cry
Habitat
SO WE NEED TO GET ITS FAN.
BUT HOW, IF IT CAN CONTROL OUR POKÉMON?
!
RAIHAN, LOOK!
YAMPER IS FIGHTING AGAINST ORANGURU ...
AND LANCELOT IS BEING CON-TROLLED.
IT CAN ONLY CONTROL ONE AT A TIME.
WE NEED TO GRAB THE FAN TOGETHER!

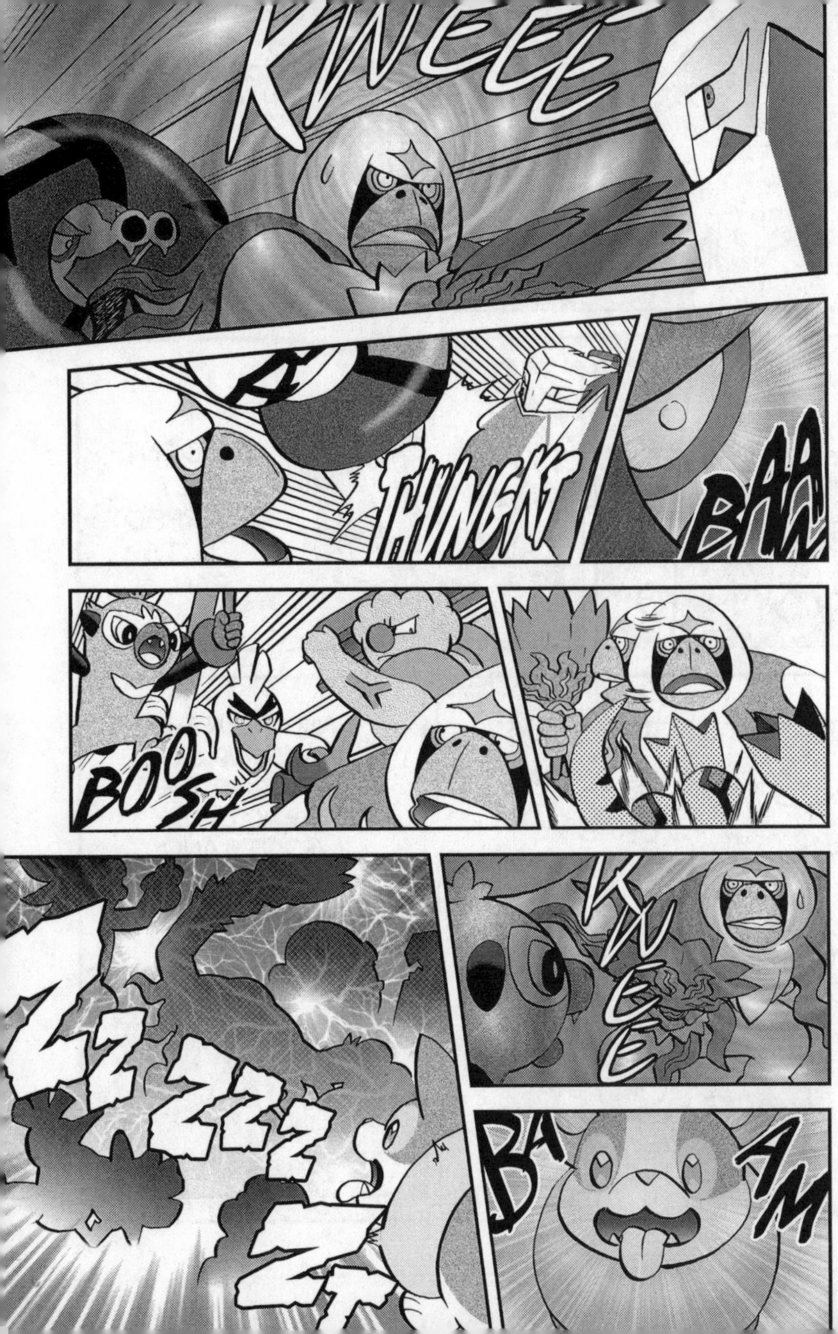
KWEEE
BAAM
THUNK
BOOSH
KWEEE
BAAM
ZZZZZZT

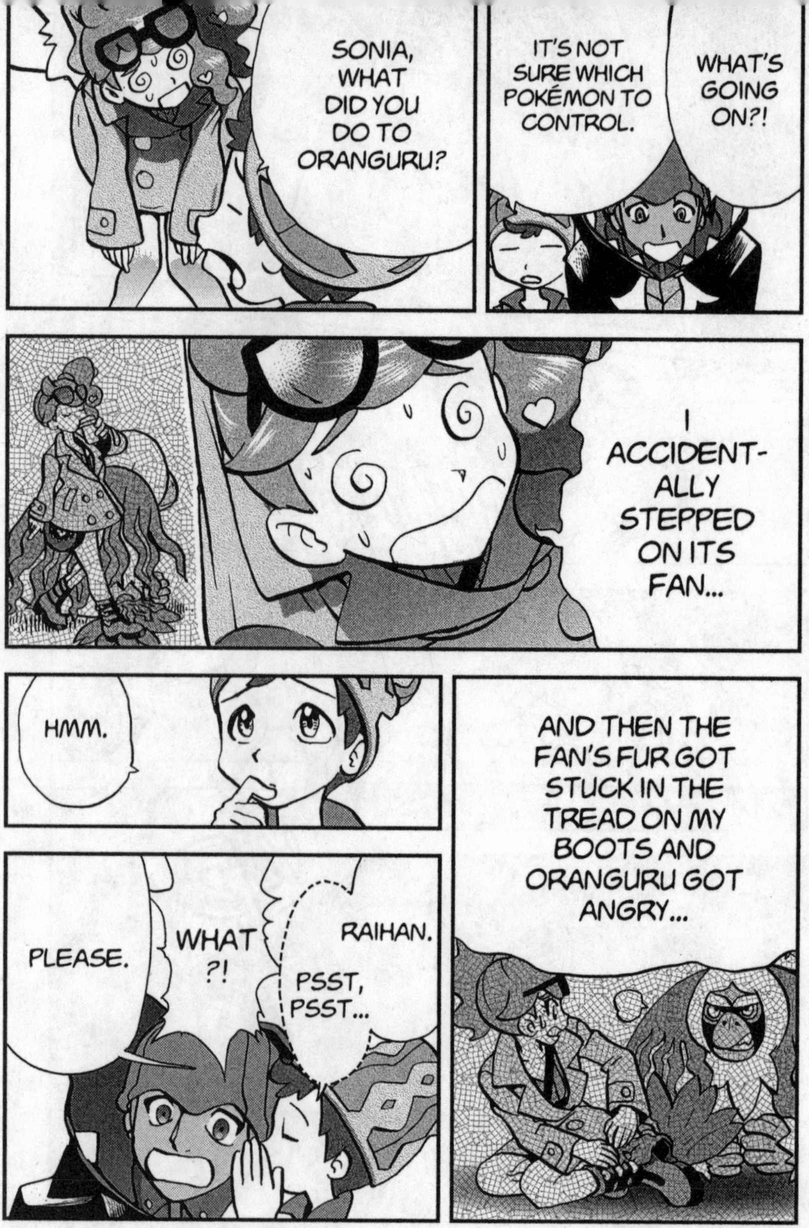
WHAT'S GOING ON?!
IT'S NOT SURE WHICH POKÉMON TO CONTROL.
SONIA, WHAT DID YOU DO TO ORANGURU?
I ACCIDENT-ALLY STEPPED ON ITS FAN...
AND THEN THE FAN'S FUR GOT STUCK IN THE TREAD ON MY BOOTS AND ORANGURU GOT ANGRY...
HMM.
RAIHAN.
PSST, PSST...
WHAT ?!
PLEASE.

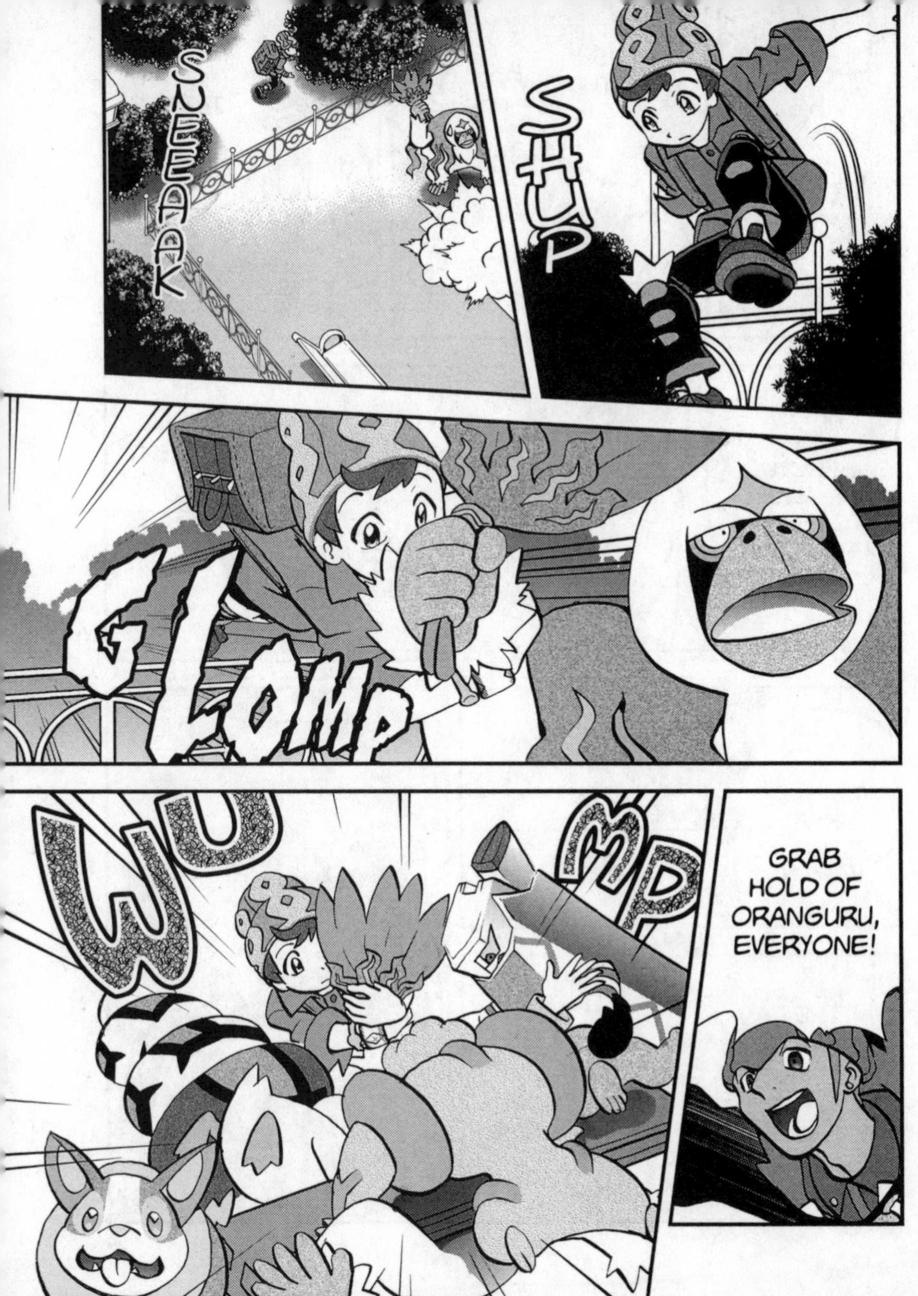
SHUP
SNEEAK
GLOMP
GRAB HOLD OF ORANGURU, EVERYONE!
WUMP

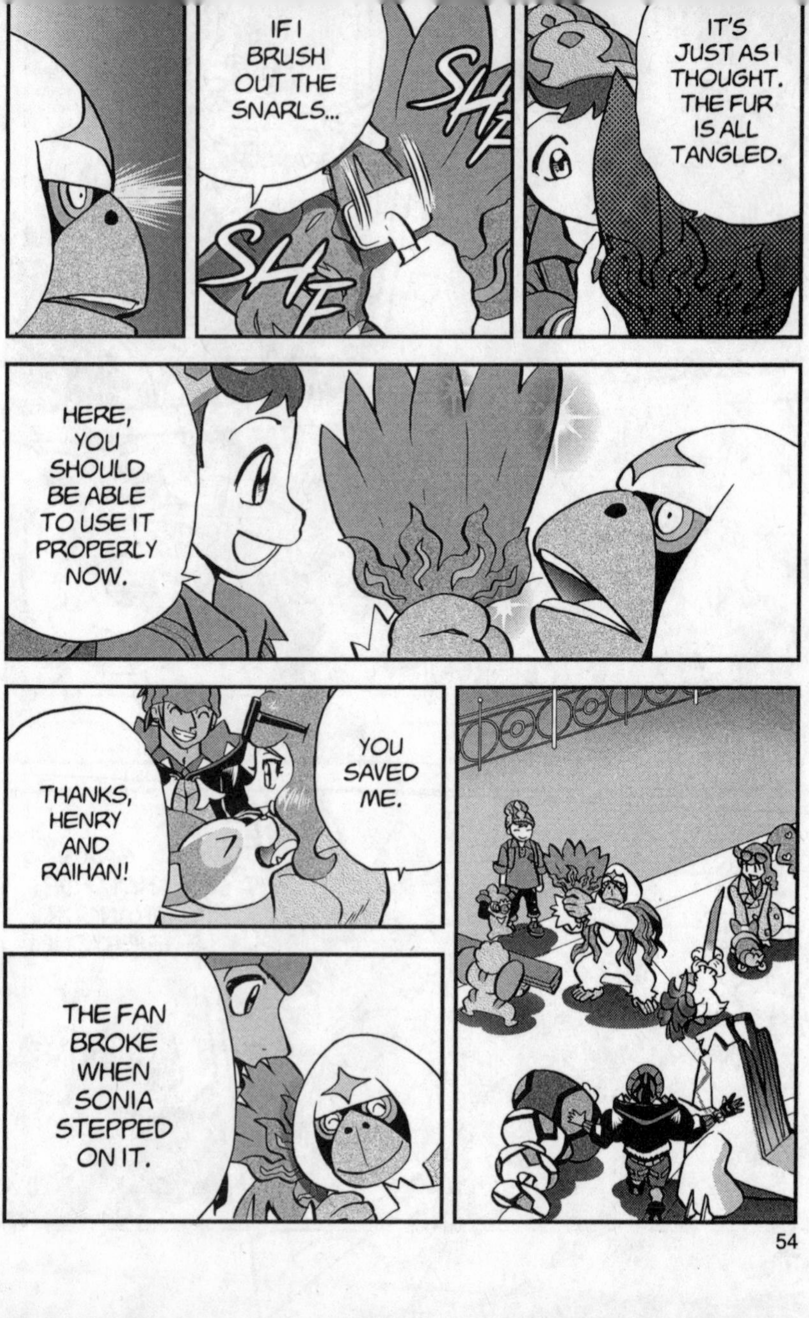
IT'S JUST AS I THOUGHT. THE FUR IS ALL TANGLED.
IF I BRUSH OUT THE SNARLS...
SHF
SHF
HERE, YOU SHOULD BE ABLE TO USE IT PROPERLY NOW.
YOU SAVED ME.
THANKS, HENRY AND RAIHAN!
THE FAN BROKE WHEN SONIA STEPPED ON IT.

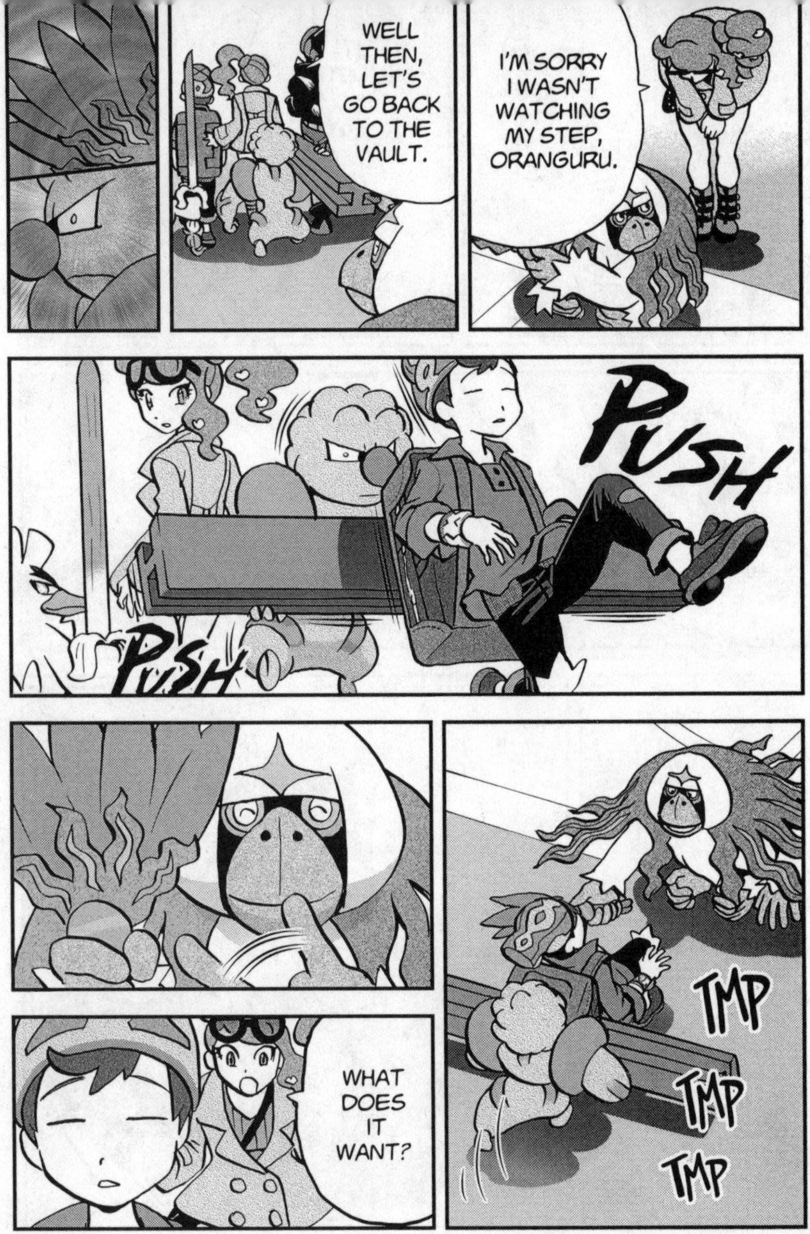
I'M SORRY I WASN'T WATCHING MY STEP, ORANGURU.
WELL THEN, LET'S GO BACK TO THE VAULT.
PUSH
PUSH
TMP
TMP
TMP
WHAT DOES IT WANT?

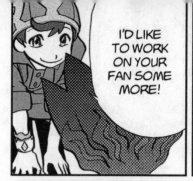

I THINK IT LIKED HOW I FIXED ITS FAN!
IT WANTS TO JOIN MY TEAM.
I'D LIKE TO WORK ON YOUR FAN SOME MORE!
SHUUP!!!
NICE TO MEET YOU.
I'LL CALL YOU...
...FAN-GURU.
SORRY AGAIN. NOW COME WITH ME!
SHE SEEMS TO HAVE MADE A DISCOVERY.

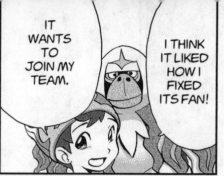

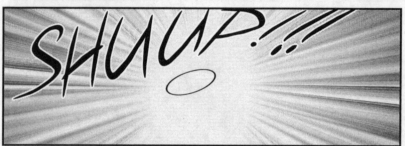

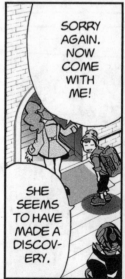

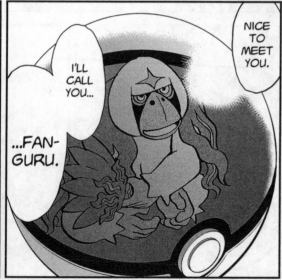

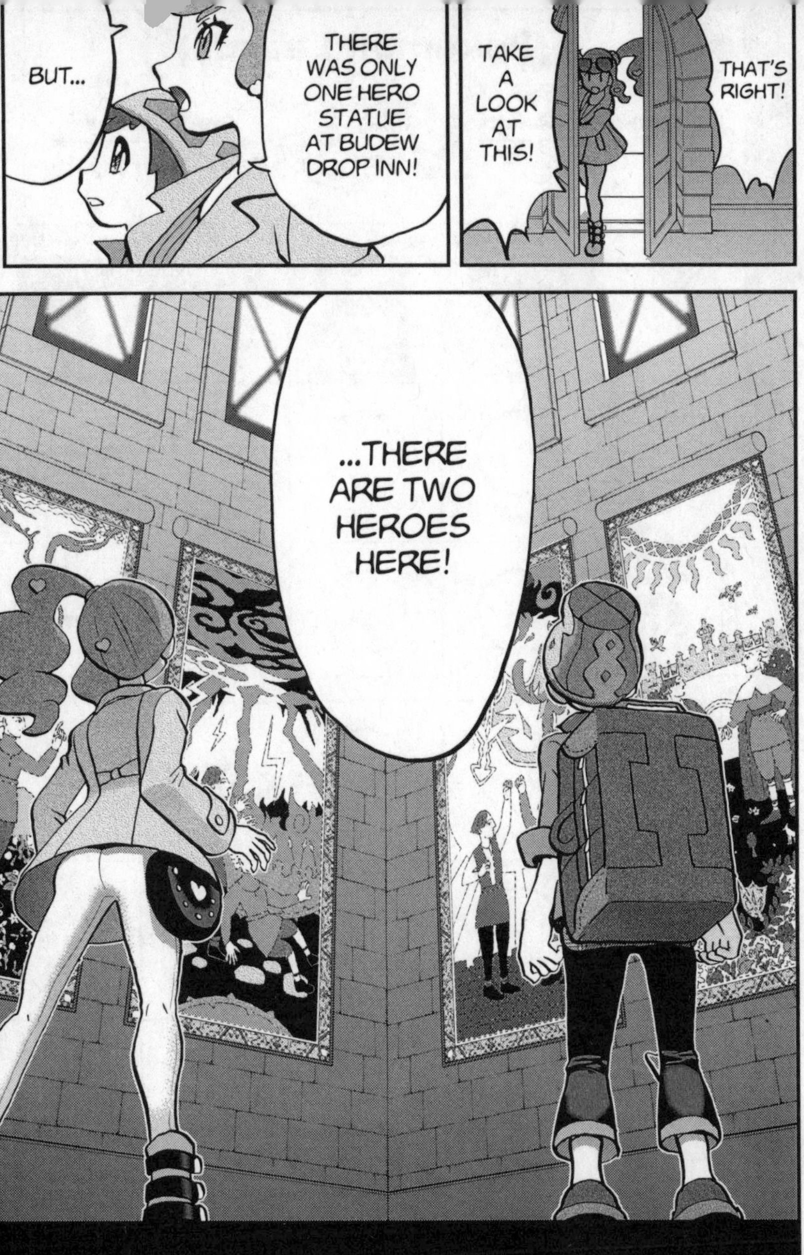
THAT'S RIGHT!
TAKE A LOOK AT THIS!
THERE WAS ONLY ONE HERO STATUE AT BUDEW DROP INN!
BUT...
...THERE ARE TWO HEROES HERE!

(Pokémon League)

Challenger's Results — **Gym Challenge**

○: Victory
●: Defeat

(2–0): Remaining Pokémon

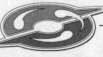

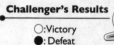

		TURFFIELD STADIUM MILO	HULBURY STADIUM NESSA	MOTOSTOKE STADIUM KABU	STOW-ON-SIDE STADIUM [redacted]
ENDORSED BY THE CHAMPION	HENRY	○ (2–0)	○ (2–0)	○ (3–0)	CURRENTLY APPLYING
ENDORSED BY THE CHAMPION	CASEY	○ (1–0)	○ (1–0)	○ (1–0)	■■■
ENDORSED BY THE CHAIRMAN	BEDE	○ (2–0)	○ (1–0)	CURRENTLY CHALLENGING	■■■
NORMAL CHALLENGERS	HOP	○ (1–0)	○ (2–0)	○ (1–0)	■■■
NORMAL CHALLENGERS	MARNIE	○ (1–0)	○ (1–0)	○ (2–0)	■■■
NORMAL CHALLENGERS	[redacted]	●	■■■	■■■	■■■

Adventure 13 Glittering!! The Tapestry in the Vault

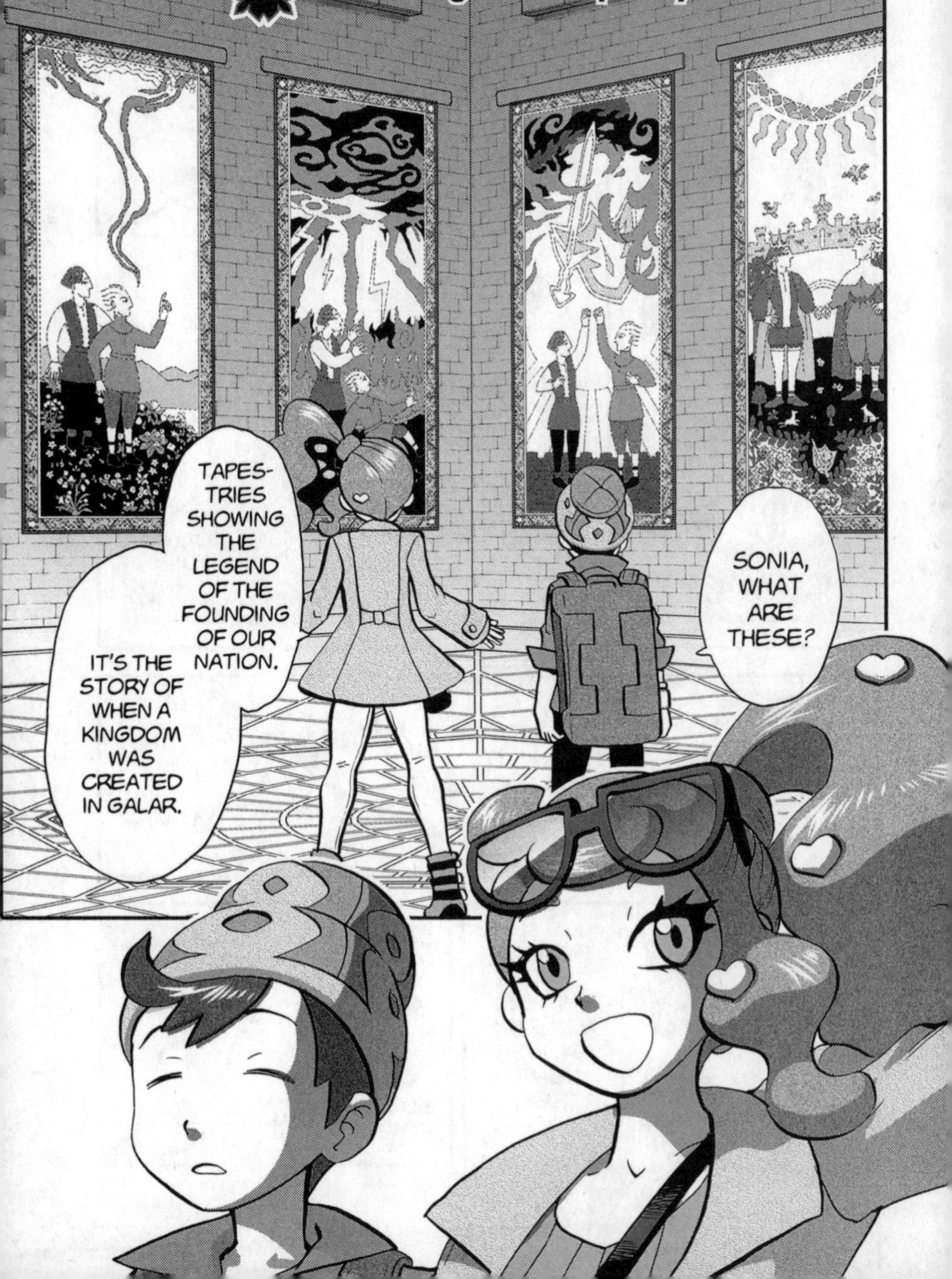
SONIA, WHAT ARE THESE?
TAPES-TRIES SHOWING THE LEGEND OF THE FOUNDING OF OUR NATION.
IT'S THE STORY OF WHEN A KINGDOM WAS CREATED IN GALAR.

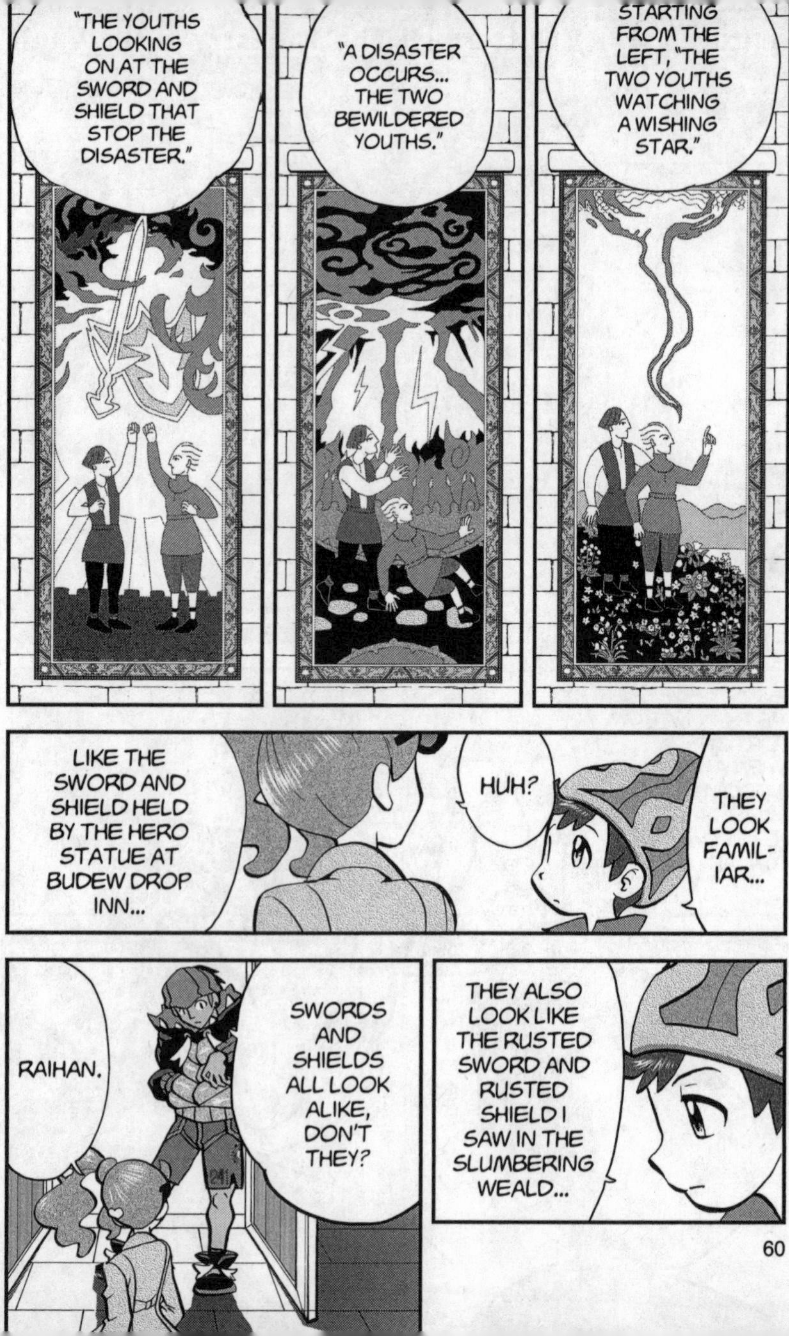
STARTING FROM THE LEFT, "THE TWO YOUTHS WATCHING A WISHING STAR."
"A DISASTER OCCURS... THE TWO BEWILDERED YOUTHS."
"THE YOUTHS LOOKING ON AT THE SWORD AND SHIELD THAT STOP THE DISASTER."
THEY LOOK FAMIL-IAR...
HUH?
LIKE THE SWORD AND SHIELD HELD BY THE HERO STATUE AT BUDEW DROP INN...
THEY ALSO LOOK LIKE THE RUSTED SWORD AND RUSTED SHIELD I SAW IN THE SLUMBERING WEALD...
SWORDS AND SHIELDS ALL LOOK ALIKE, DON'T THEY?
RAIHAN.

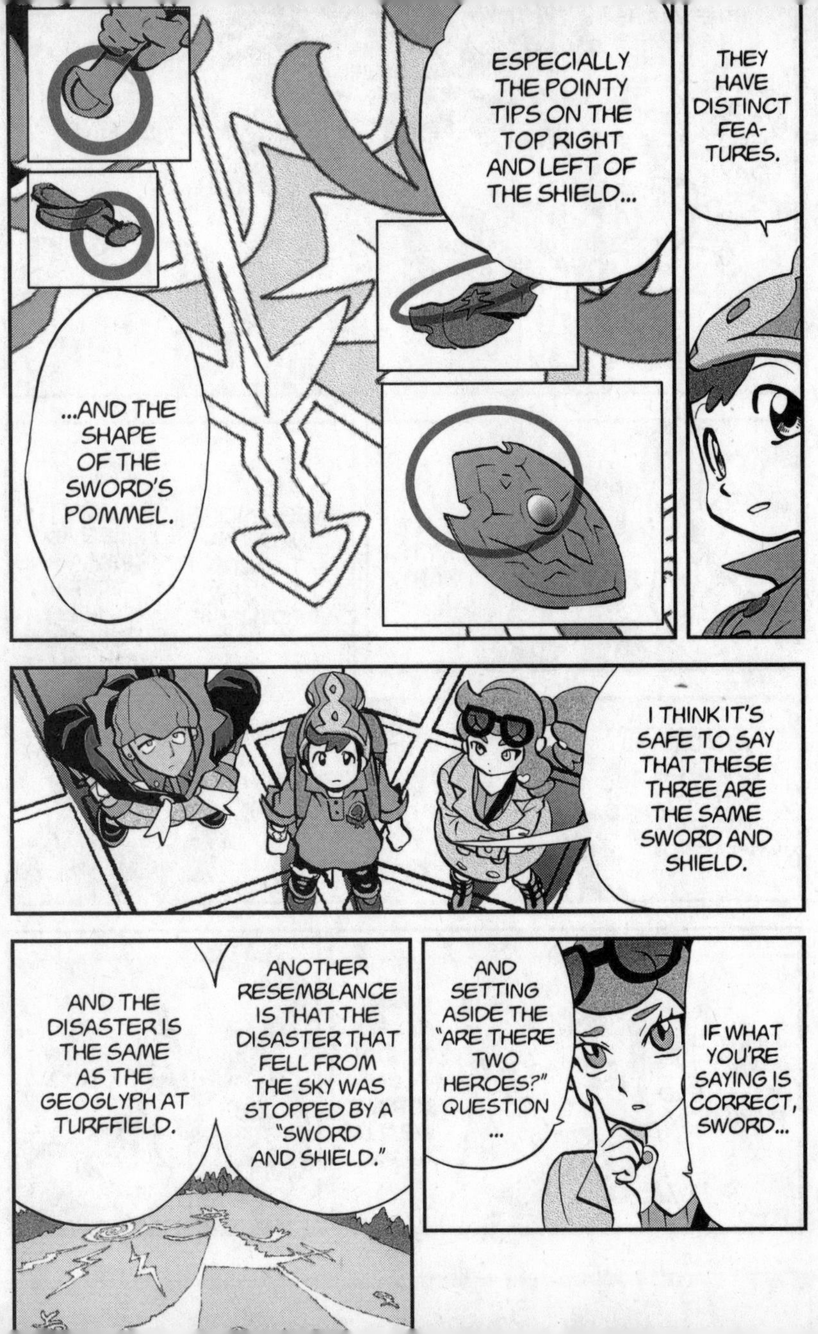

THEY HAVE DISTINCT FEA-TURES.
ESPECIALLY THE POINTY TIPS ON THE TOP RIGHT AND LEFT OF THE SHIELD...
...AND THE SHAPE OF THE SWORD'S POMMEL.
I THINK IT'S SAFE TO SAY THAT THESE THREE ARE THE SAME SWORD AND SHIELD.
IF WHAT YOU'RE SAYING IS CORRECT, SWORD...
AND SETTING ASIDE THE "ARE THERE TWO HEROES?" QUESTION ...
ANOTHER RESEMBLANCE IS THAT THE DISASTER THAT FELL FROM THE SKY WAS STOPPED BY A "SWORD AND SHIELD."
AND THE DISASTER IS THE SAME AS THE GEOGLYPH AT TURFFIELD.

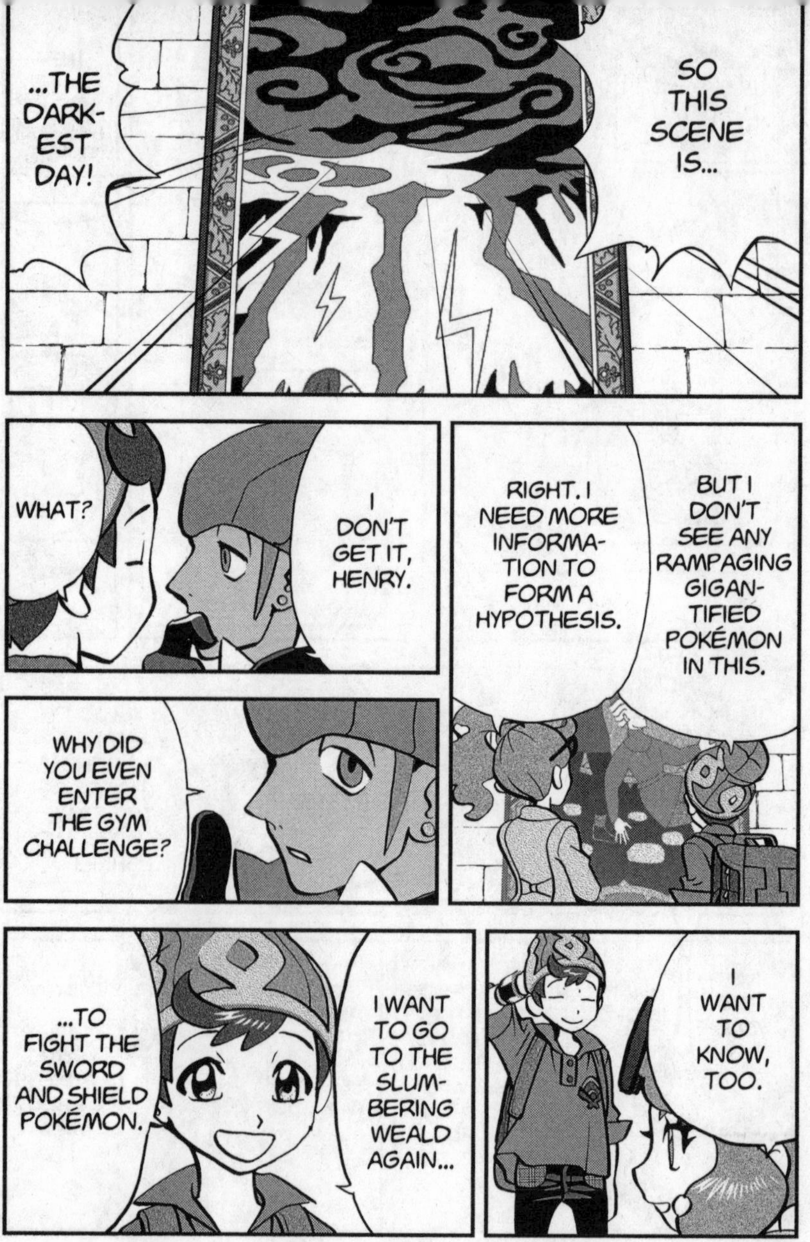
SO THIS SCENE IS...
...THE DARKEST DAY!
BUT I DON'T SEE ANY RAMPAGING GIGANTIFIED POKÉMON IN THIS.
RIGHT. I NEED MORE INFORMATION TO FORM A HYPOTHESIS.
I DON'T GET IT, HENRY.
WHAT?
WHY DID YOU EVEN ENTER THE GYM CHALLENGE?
I WANT TO KNOW, TOO.
I WANT TO GO TO THE SLUMBERING WEALD AGAIN...
...TO FIGHT THE SWORD AND SHIELD POKÉMON.

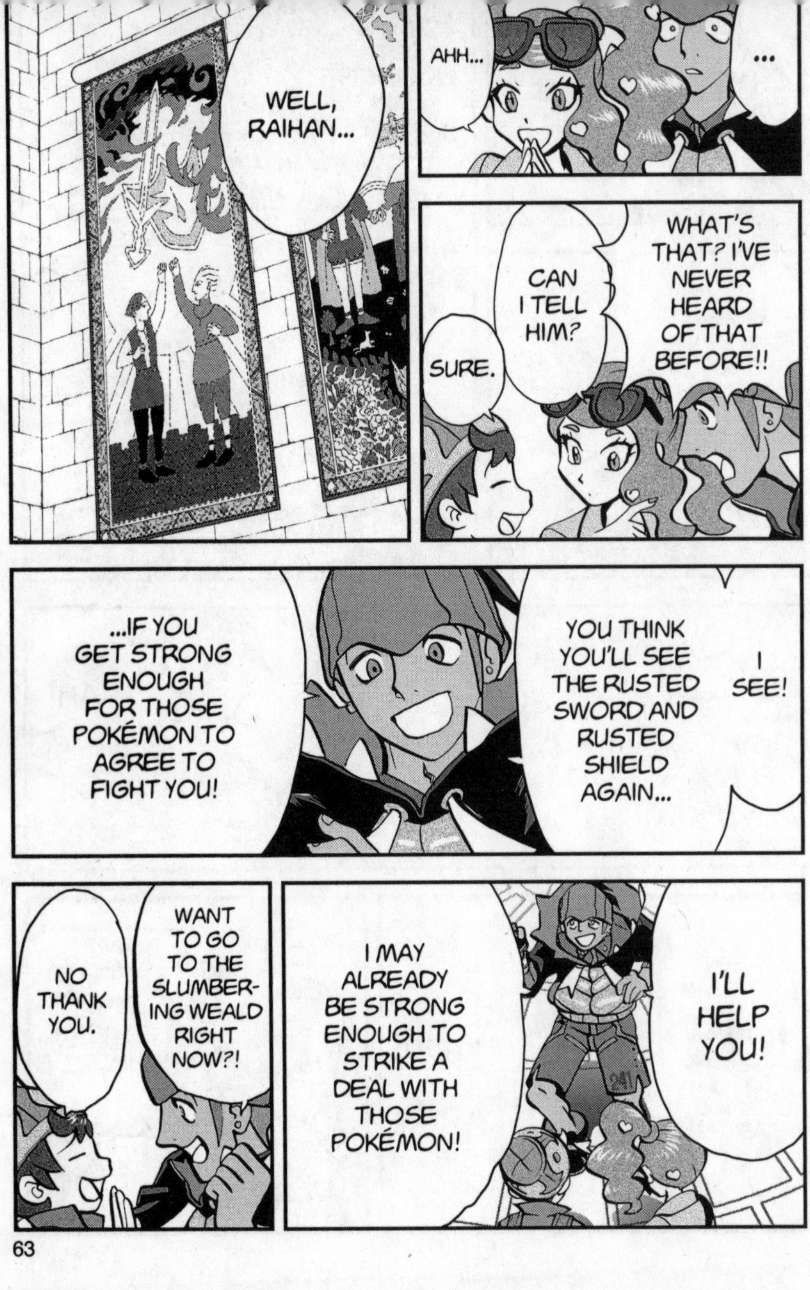
...
AHH...
WHAT'S THAT? I'VE NEVER HEARD OF THAT BEFORE!!
CAN I TELL HIM?
SURE.
WELL, RAIHAN...
I SEE!
YOU THINK YOU'LL SEE THE RUSTED SWORD AND RUSTED SHIELD AGAIN...
...IF YOU GET STRONG ENOUGH FOR THOSE POKÉMON TO AGREE TO FIGHT YOU!
I'LL HELP YOU!
I MAY ALREADY BE STRONG ENOUGH TO STRIKE A DEAL WITH THOSE POKÉMON!
WANT TO GO TO THE SLUMBER-ING WEALD RIGHT NOW?!
NO THANK YOU.

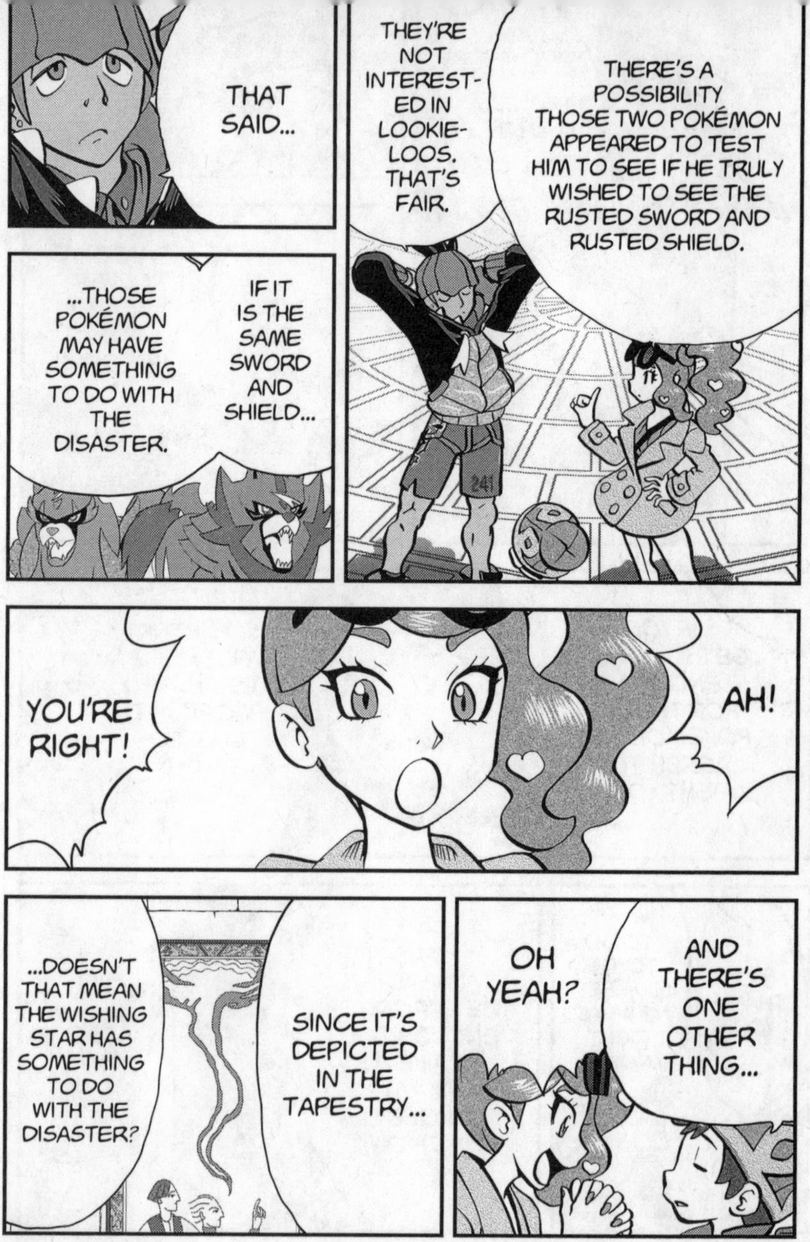
THERE'S A POSSIBILITY THOSE TWO POKÉMON APPEARED TO TEST HIM TO SEE IF HE TRULY WISHED TO SEE THE RUSTED SWORD AND RUSTED SHIELD.
THEY'RE NOT INTEREST-ED IN LOOKIE-LOOS. THAT'S FAIR.
THAT SAID...
IF IT IS THE SAME SWORD AND SHIELD...
...THOSE POKÉMON MAY HAVE SOMETHING TO DO WITH THE DISASTER.
AH!
YOU'RE RIGHT!
AND THERE'S ONE OTHER THING...
OH YEAH?
SINCE IT'S DEPICTED IN THE TAPESTRY...
...DOESN'T THAT MEAN THE WISHING STAR HAS SOMETHING TO DO WITH THE DISASTER?

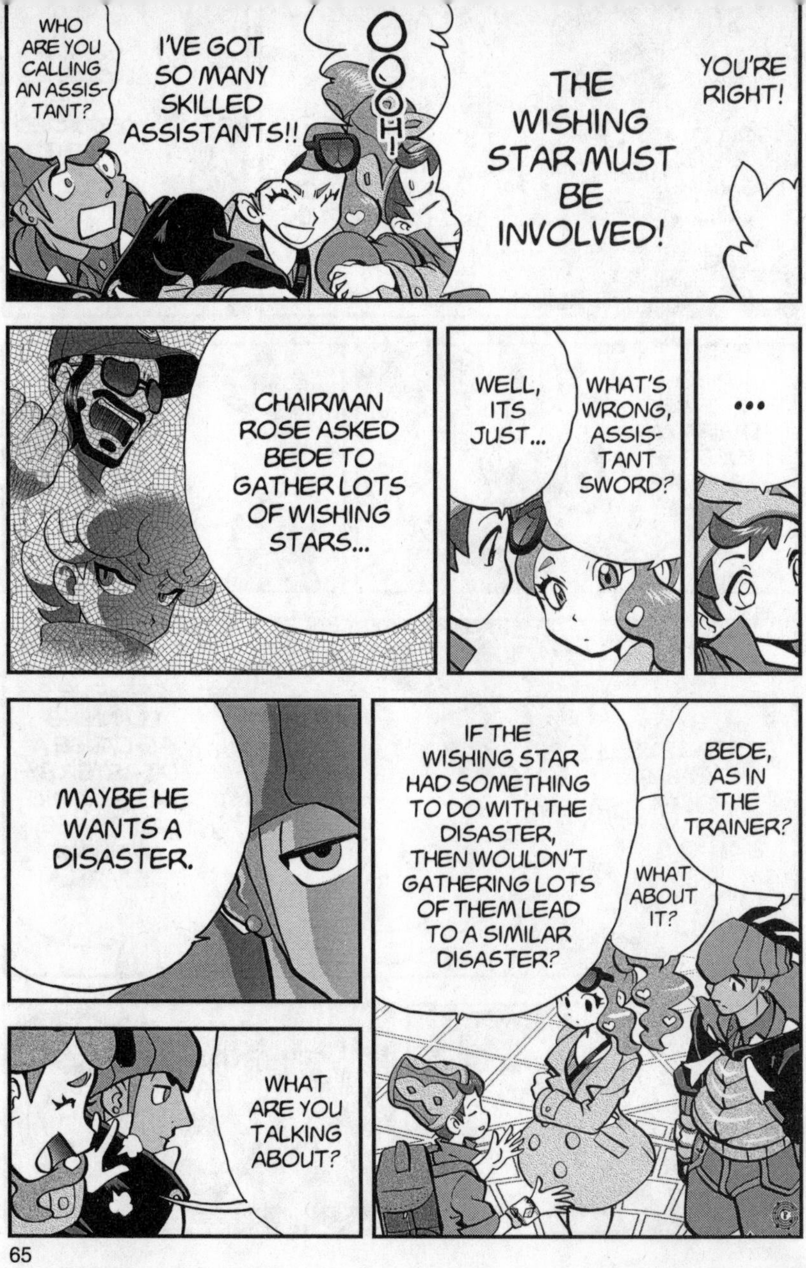
YOU'RE RIGHT!
THE WISHING STAR MUST BE INVOLVED!
OOOOH!
I'VE GOT SO MANY SKILLED ASSISTANTS!!
WHO ARE YOU CALLING AN ASSISTANT?
...
WHAT'S WRONG, ASSISTANT SWORD?
WELL, ITS JUST...
CHAIRMAN ROSE ASKED BEDE TO GATHER LOTS OF WISHING STARS...
BEDE, AS IN THE TRAINER?
WHAT ABOUT IT?
IF THE WISHING STAR HAD SOMETHING TO DO WITH THE DISASTER, THEN WOULDN'T GATHERING LOTS OF THEM LEAD TO A SIMILAR DISASTER?
MAYBE HE WANTS A DISASTER.
WHAT ARE YOU TALKING ABOUT?

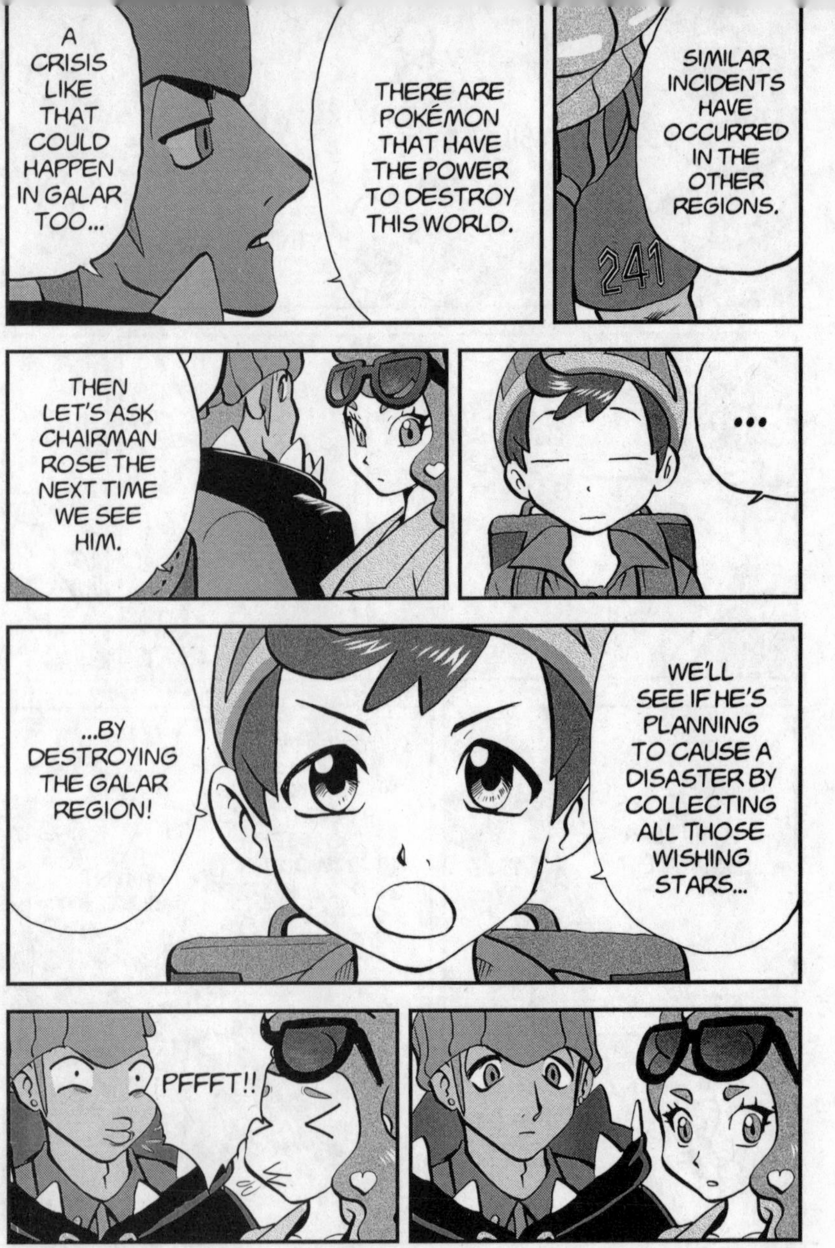
SIMILAR INCIDENTS HAVE OCCURRED IN THE OTHER REGIONS.
THERE ARE POKÉMON THAT HAVE THE POWER TO DESTROY THIS WORLD.
A CRISIS LIKE THAT COULD HAPPEN IN GALAR TOO...
...
THEN LET'S ASK CHAIRMAN ROSE THE NEXT TIME WE SEE HIM.
WE'LL SEE IF HE'S PLANNING TO CAUSE A DISASTER BY COLLECTING ALL THOSE WISHING STARS...
...BY DESTROYING THE GALAR REGION!
PFFFT!!

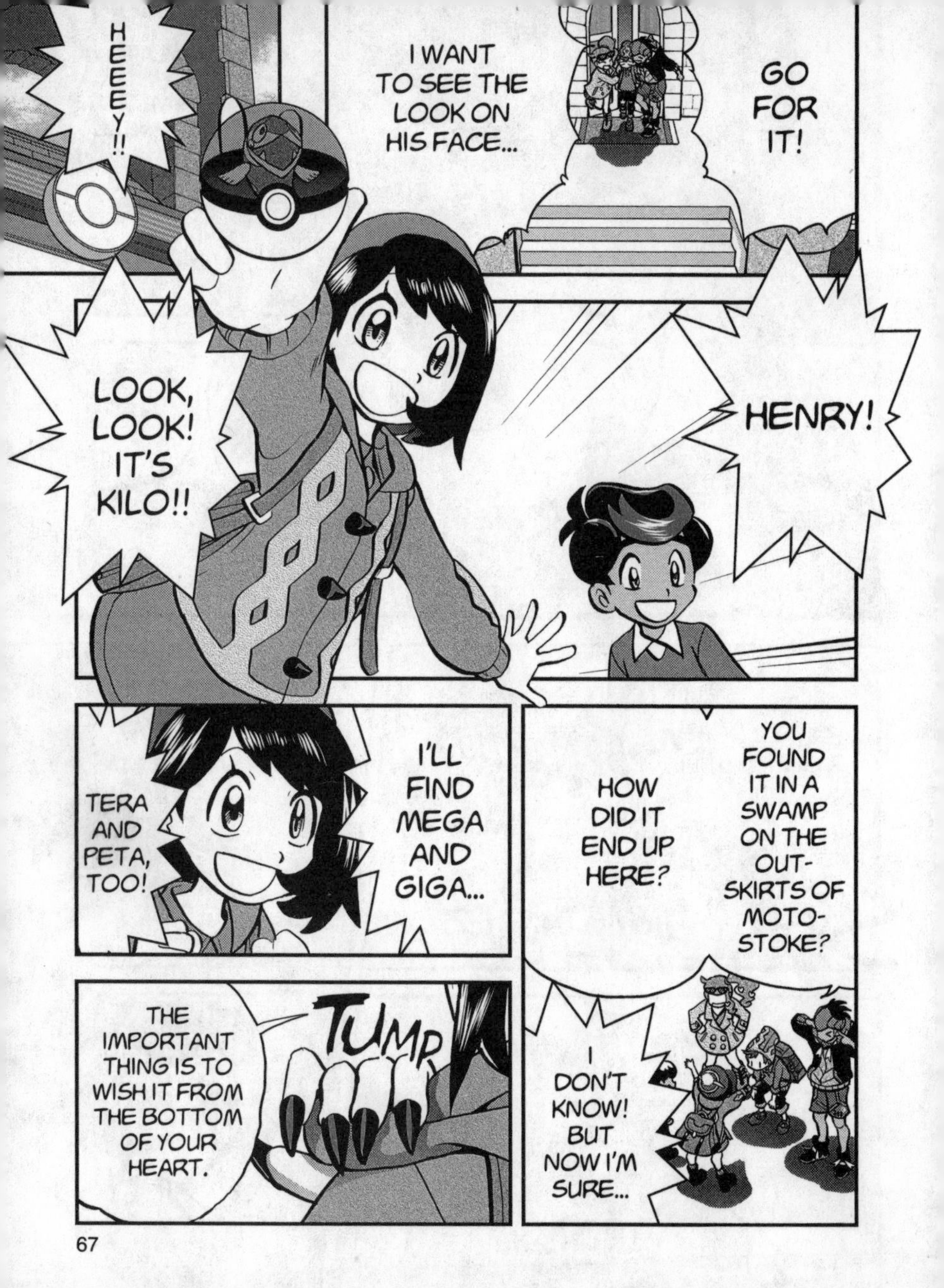
GO FOR IT!
I WANT TO SEE THE LOOK ON HIS FACE...
HEEEEY!!
HENRY!
LOOK, LOOK! IT'S KILO!!
YOU FOUND IT IN A SWAMP ON THE OUT-SKIRTS OF MOTO-STOKE?
HOW DID IT END UP HERE?
I'LL FIND MEGA AND GIGA...
TERA AND PETA, TOO!
I DON'T KNOW! BUT NOW I'M SURE...
TUMP
THE IMPORTANT THING IS TO WISH IT FROM THE BOTTOM OF YOUR HEART.

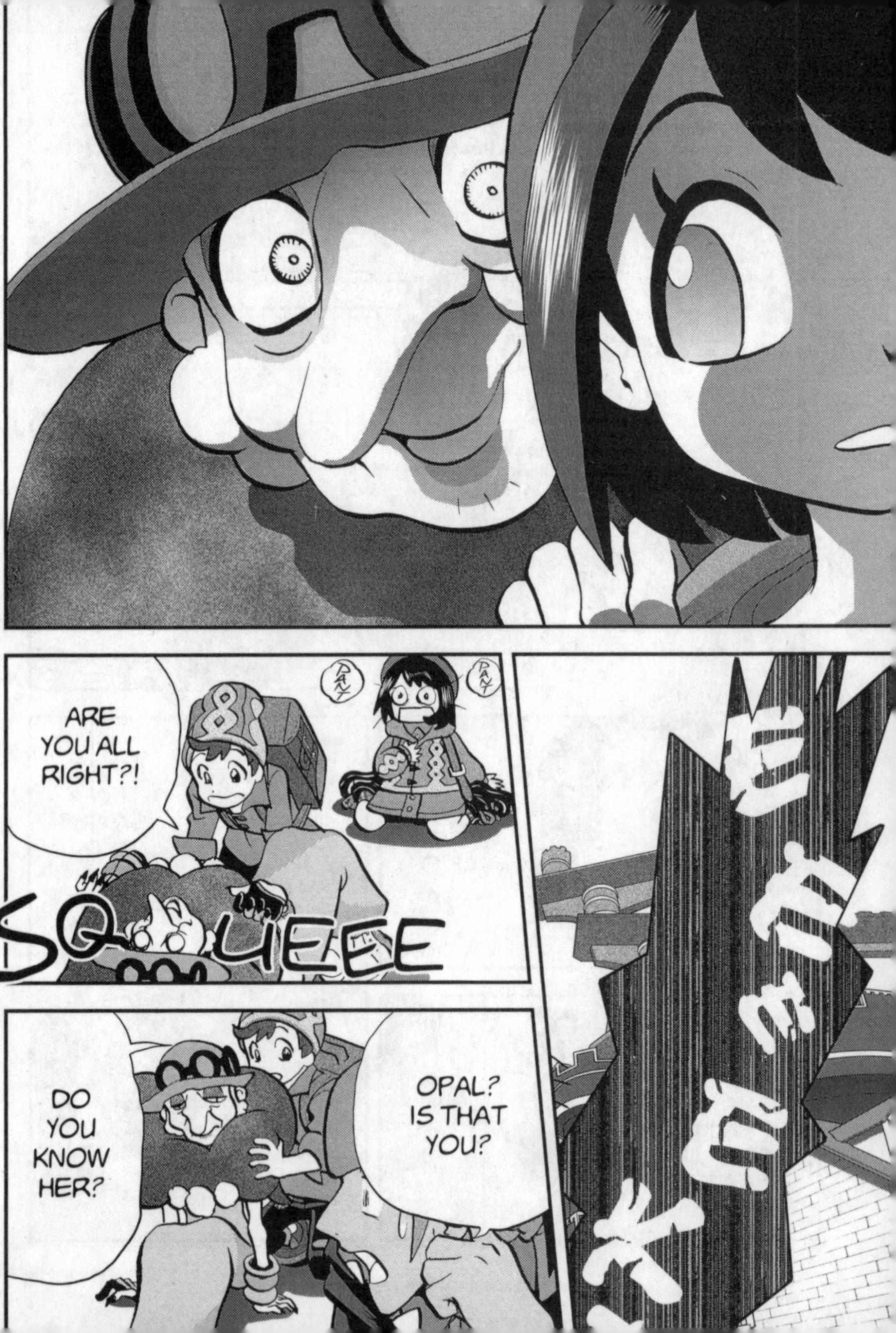
ARE YOU ALL RIGHT?!
SQUEEE
OPAL? IS THAT YOU?
DO YOU KNOW HER?

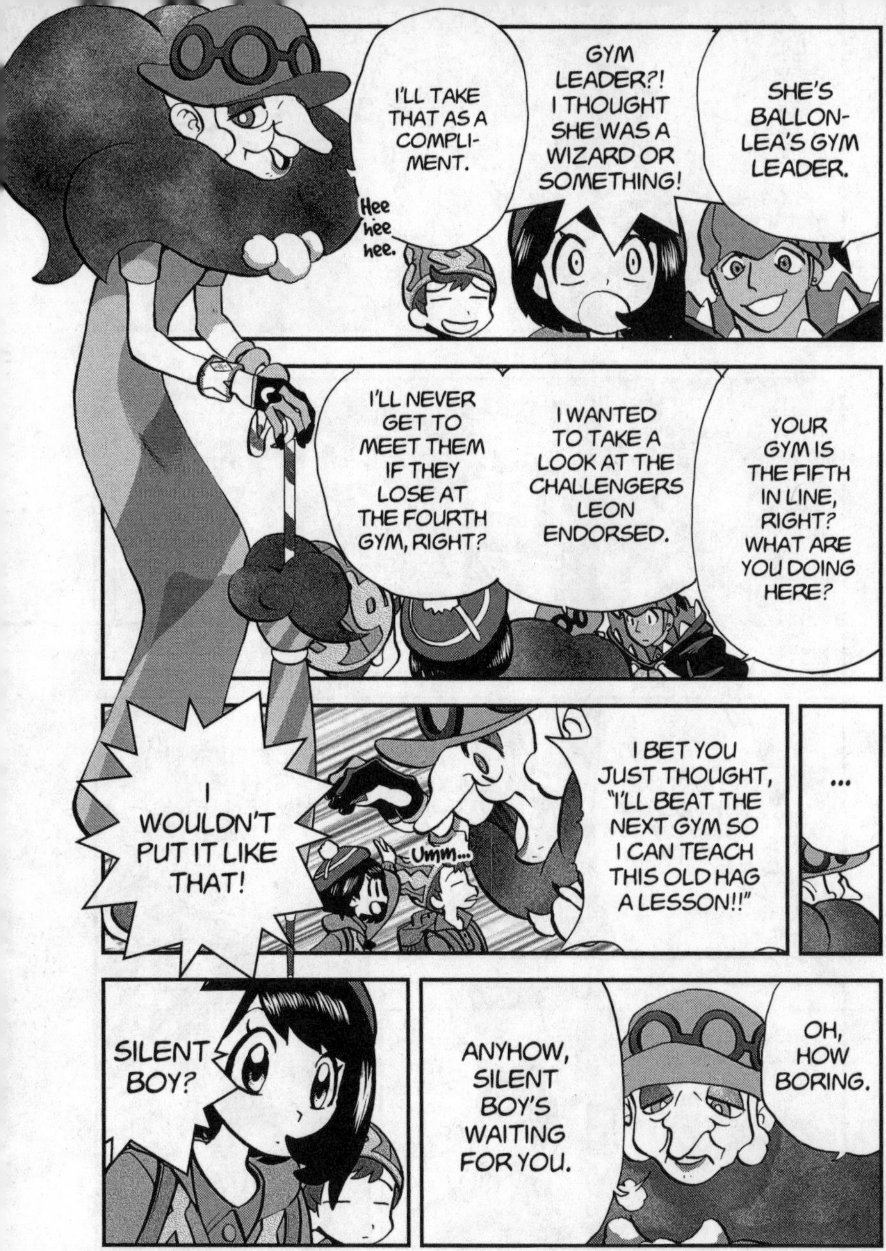
SHE'S BALLON-LEA'S GYM LEADER.
GYM LEADER?! I THOUGHT SHE WAS A WIZARD OR SOMETHING!
I'LL TAKE THAT AS A COMPLIMENT.
Hee hee hee.
YOUR GYM IS THE FIFTH IN LINE, RIGHT? WHAT ARE YOU DOING HERE?
I WANTED TO TAKE A LOOK AT THE CHALLENGERS LEON ENDORSED.
I'LL NEVER GET TO MEET THEM IF THEY LOSE AT THE FOURTH GYM, RIGHT?
...
I BET YOU JUST THOUGHT, "I'LL BEAT THE NEXT GYM SO I CAN TEACH THIS OLD HAG A LESSON!!"
Umm...
I WOULDN'T PUT IT LIKE THAT!
OH, HOW BORING.
ANYHOW, SILENT BOY'S WAITING FOR YOU.
SILENT BOY?

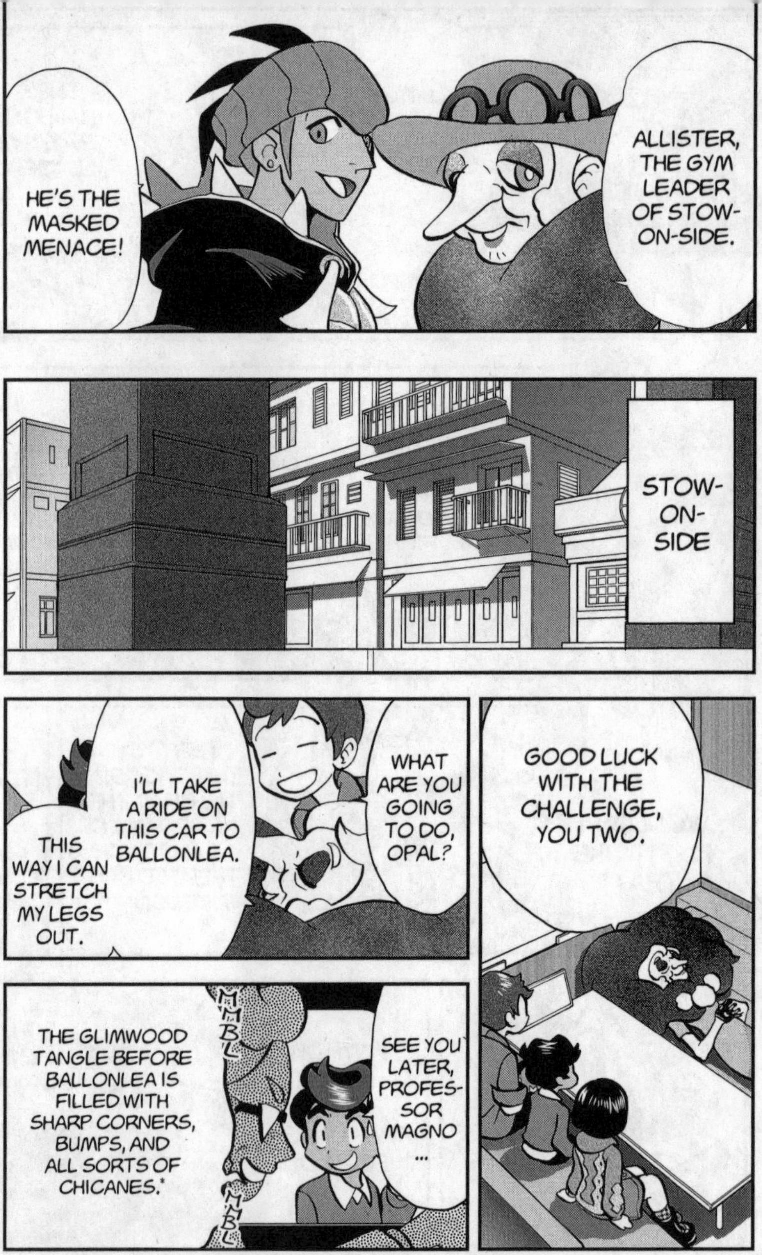
ALLISTER, THE GYM LEADER OF STOW-ON-SIDE.
HE'S THE MASKED MENACE!
STOW-ON-SIDE
GOOD LUCK WITH THE CHALLENGE, YOU TWO.
WHAT ARE YOU GOING TO DO, OPAL?
I'LL TAKE A RIDE ON THIS CAR TO BALLONLEA.
THIS WAY I CAN STRETCH MY LEGS OUT.
SEE YOU LATER, PROFESSOR MAGNO ...
MMBL
THE GLIMWOOD TANGLE BEFORE BALLONLEA IS FILLED WITH SHARP CORNERS, BUMPS, AND ALL SORTS OF CHICANES.*
MMBL

*CHICANES: SERPENTINE CURVES IN ROADS TO SLOW DOWN CARS.

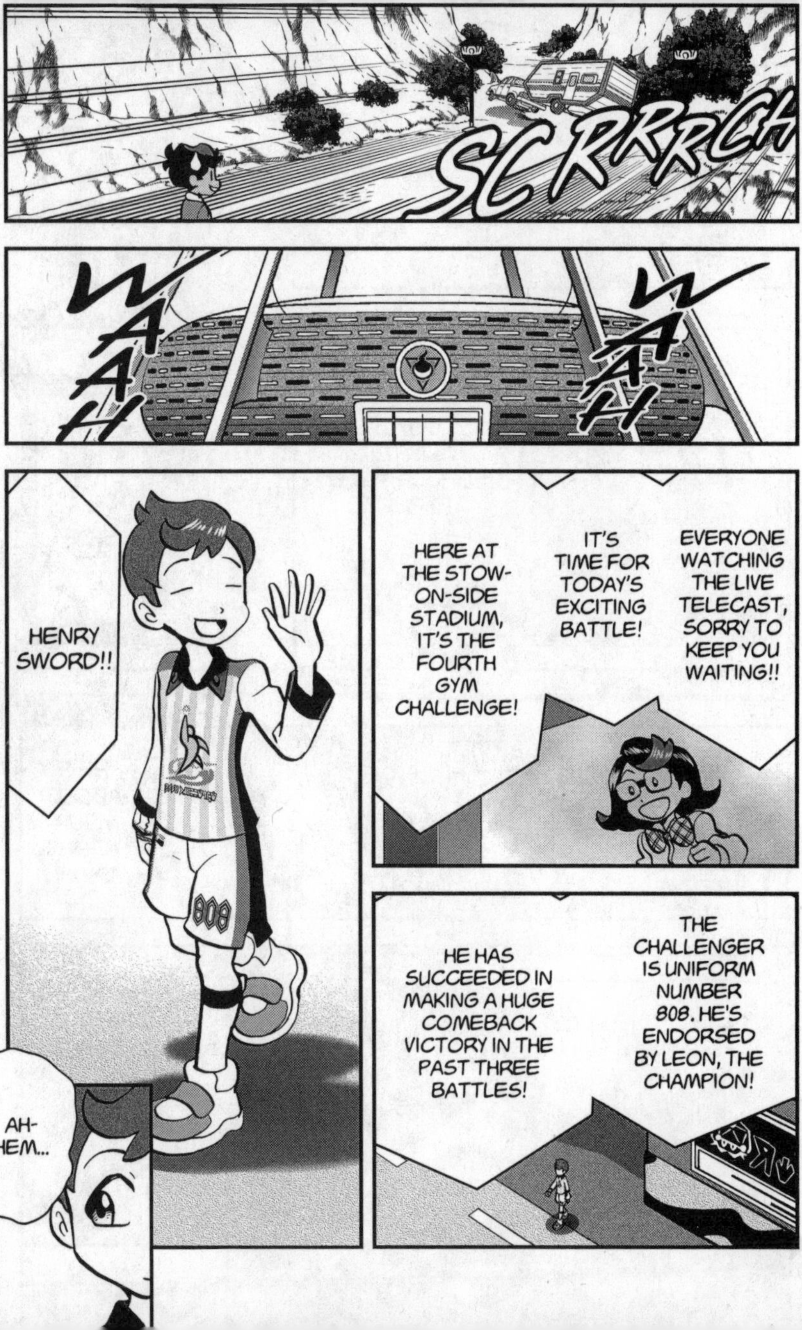
SCRRRCH
WAAH
WAAH
EVERYONE WATCHING THE LIVE TELECAST, SORRY TO KEEP YOU WAITING!!
IT'S TIME FOR TODAY'S EXCITING BATTLE!
HERE AT THE STOW-ON-SIDE STADIUM, IT'S THE FOURTH GYM CHALLENGE!
THE CHALLENGER IS UNIFORM NUMBER 808. HE'S ENDORSED BY LEON, THE CHAMPION!
HE HAS SUCCEEDED IN MAKING A HUGE COMEBACK VICTORY IN THE PAST THREE BATTLES!
HENRY SWORD!!
AH-HEM...

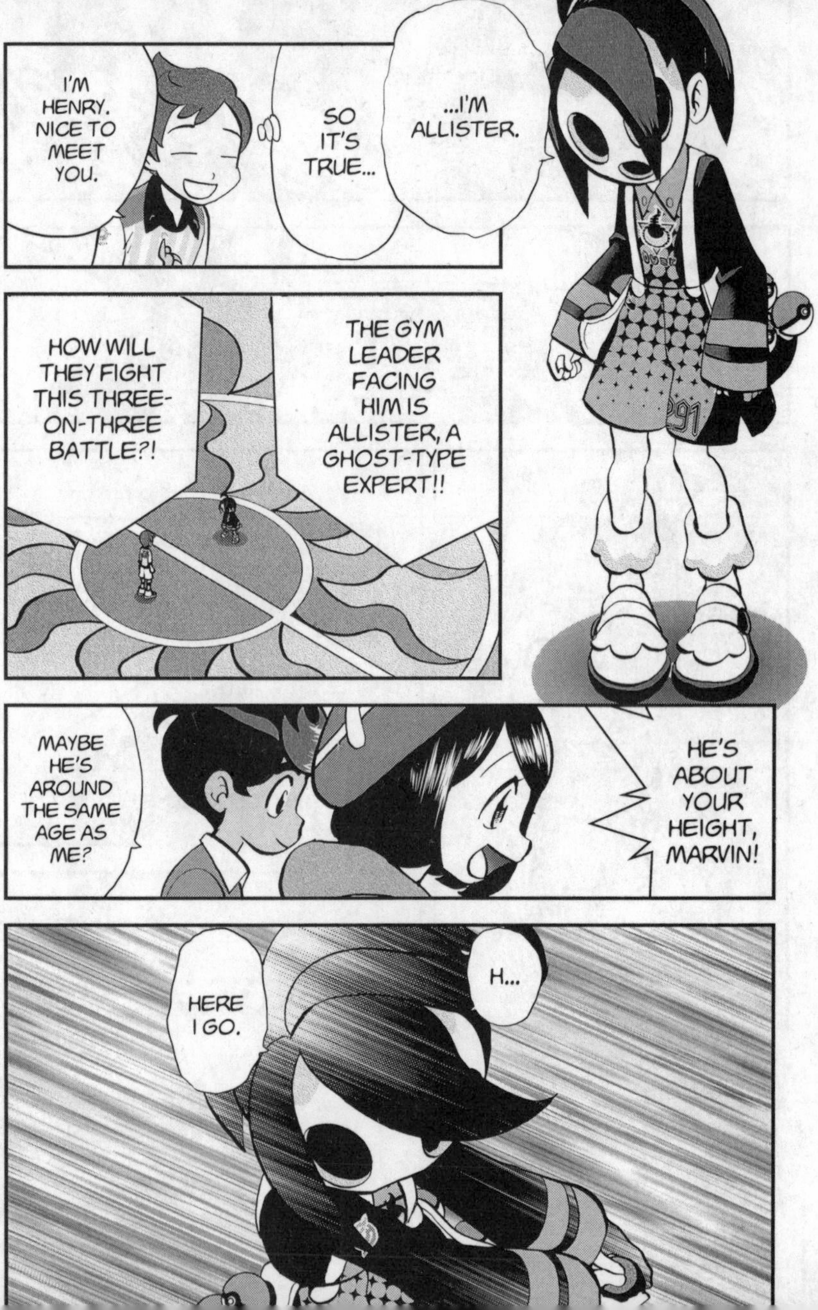
...I'M ALLISTER.
SO IT'S TRUE...
I'M HENRY. NICE TO MEET YOU.
THE GYM LEADER FACING HIM IS ALLISTER, A GHOST-TYPE EXPERT!!
HOW WILL THEY FIGHT THIS THREE-ON-THREE BATTLE?!
HE'S ABOUT YOUR HEIGHT, MARVIN!
MAYBE HE'S AROUND THE SAME AGE AS ME?
H...
HERE I GO.

A GALAR-IAN YAMASK!

COULDN'T HELP MYSELF...

OUT OF THE DUSK BALL CAME YAMASK! YEAH, MAN!

LANCE-LOT!

No. 327 Yamask

Spirit Pokémon

Type:	
Height:	1'08"
Weight:	3.3 lbs
Number Battled:	

Galarian Form

It's said that this Pokémon was formed when an ancient clay tablet was drawn to a vengeful spirit.

BOM!

UH-HUH! IT'S A GROUND AND A GHOST TYPE!

THEN IT'S NOT JUST A GHOST TYPE?

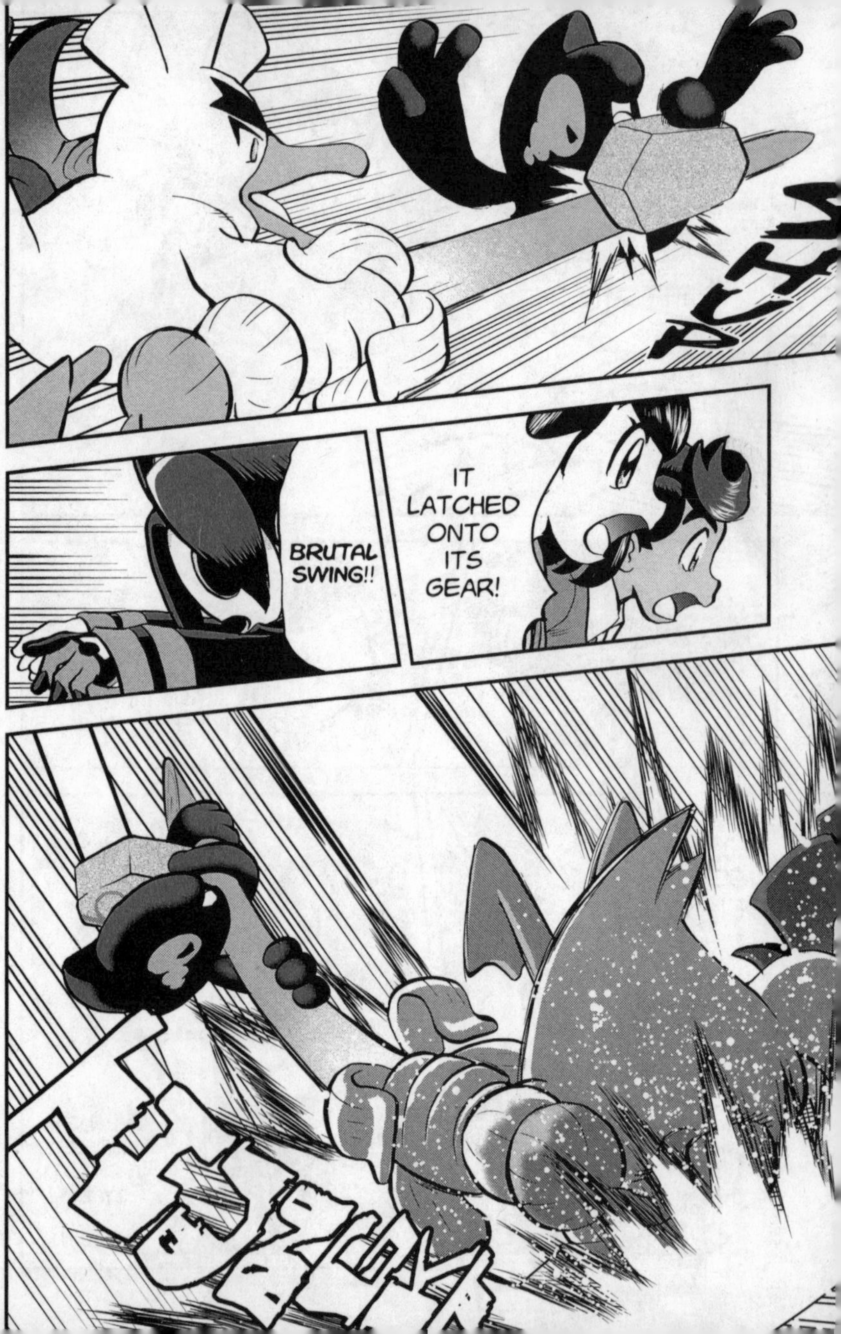
IT LATCHED ONTO ITS GEAR!
BRUTAL SWING!!

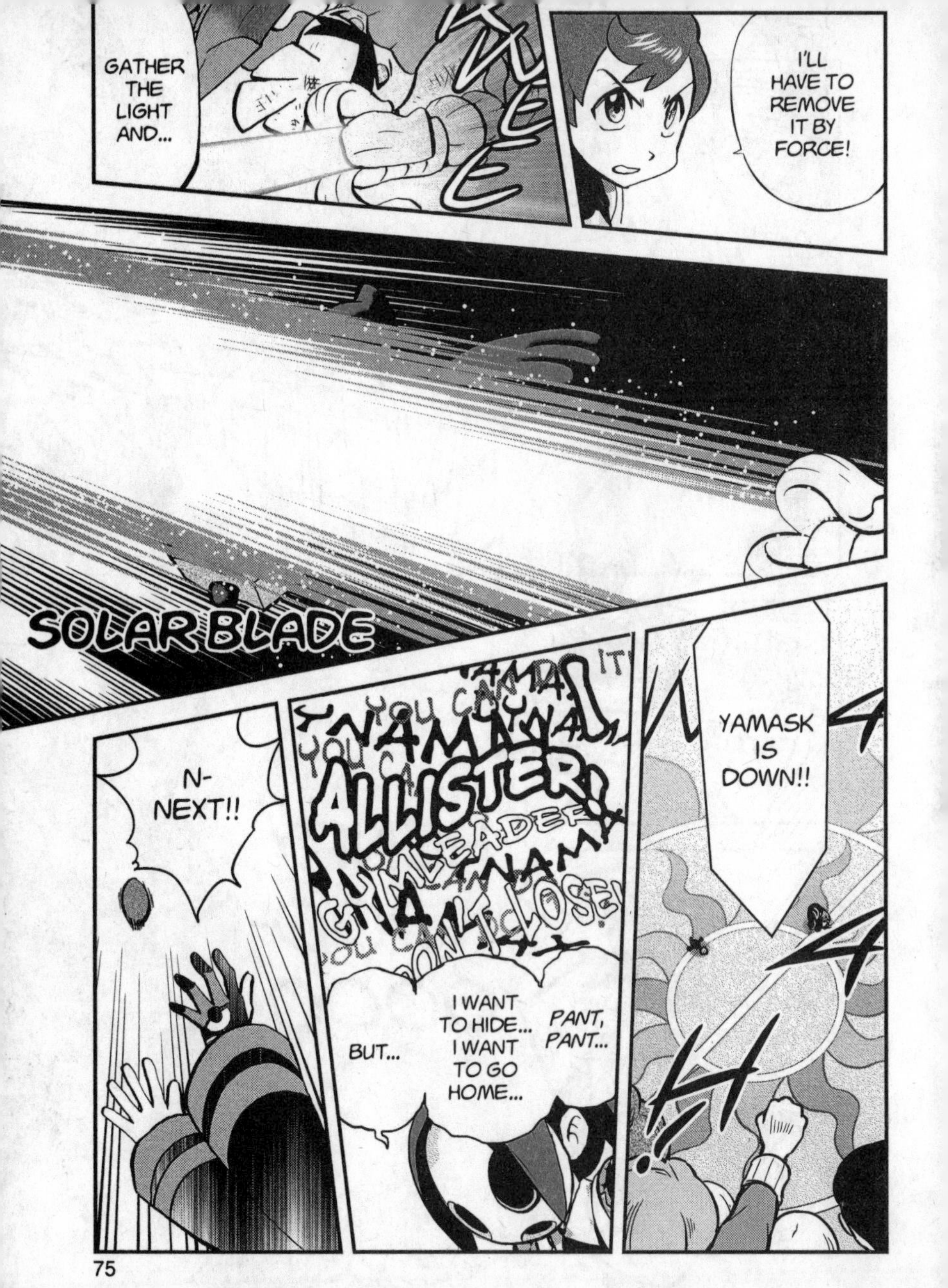
I'LL HAVE TO REMOVE IT BY FORCE!
GATHER THE LIGHT AND...
SOLAR BLADE
YAMASK IS DOWN!!
ALLISTER!
PANT, PANT...
I WANT TO HIDE... I WANT TO GO HOME...
BUT...
N- NEXT!!

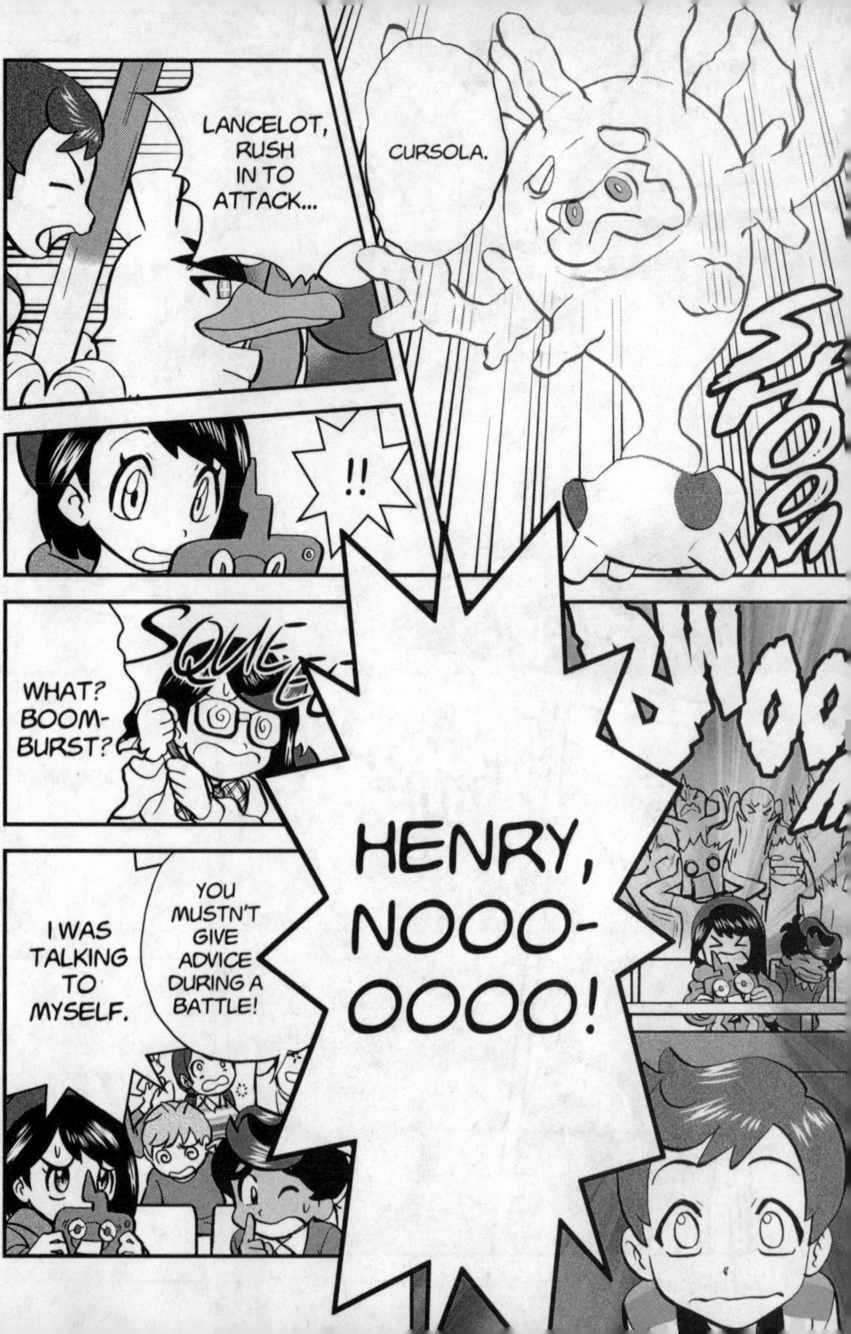
CURSOLA.
SHOOM
LANCELOT, RUSH IN TO ATTACK...
!!
BWOOM
HENRY, NOOO-OOOO!
SQUEE
WHAT? BOOM-BURST?
YOU MUSTN'T GIVE ADVICE DURING A BATTLE!
I WAS TALKING TO MYSELF.

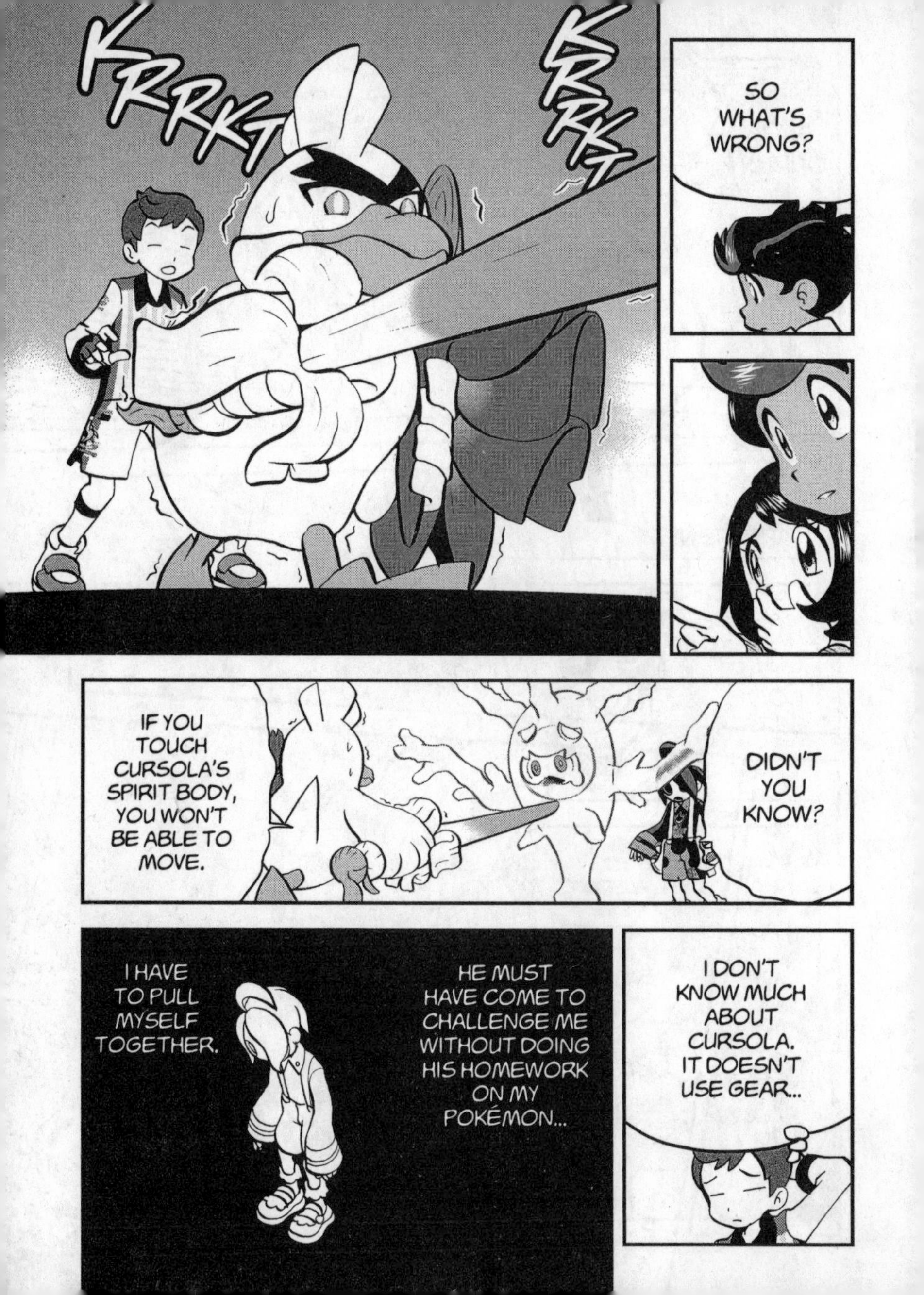
SO WHAT'S WRONG?
KRRKT
KRRKT
DIDN'T YOU KNOW?
IF YOU TOUCH CURSOLA'S SPIRIT BODY, YOU WON'T BE ABLE TO MOVE.
I DON'T KNOW MUCH ABOUT CURSOLA. IT DOESN'T USE GEAR...
HE MUST HAVE COME TO CHALLENGE ME WITHOUT DOING HIS HOMEWORK ON MY POKÉMON...
I HAVE TO PULL MYSELF TOGETHER.

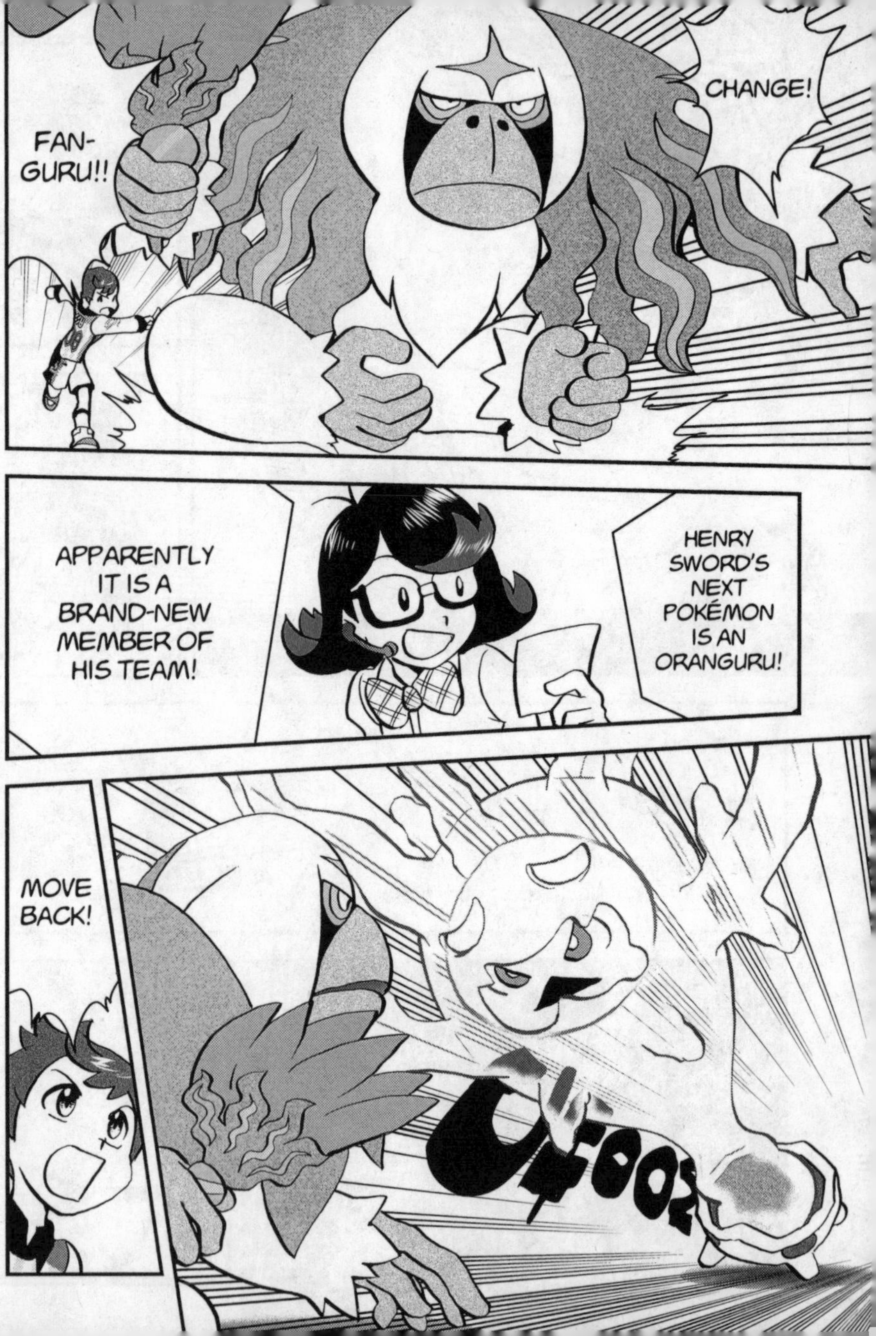
CHANGE!
FAN-GURU!!
HENRY SWORD'S NEXT POKéMON IS AN ORANGURU!
APPARENTLY IT IS A BRAND-NEW MEMBER OF HIS TEAM!
MOVE BACK!

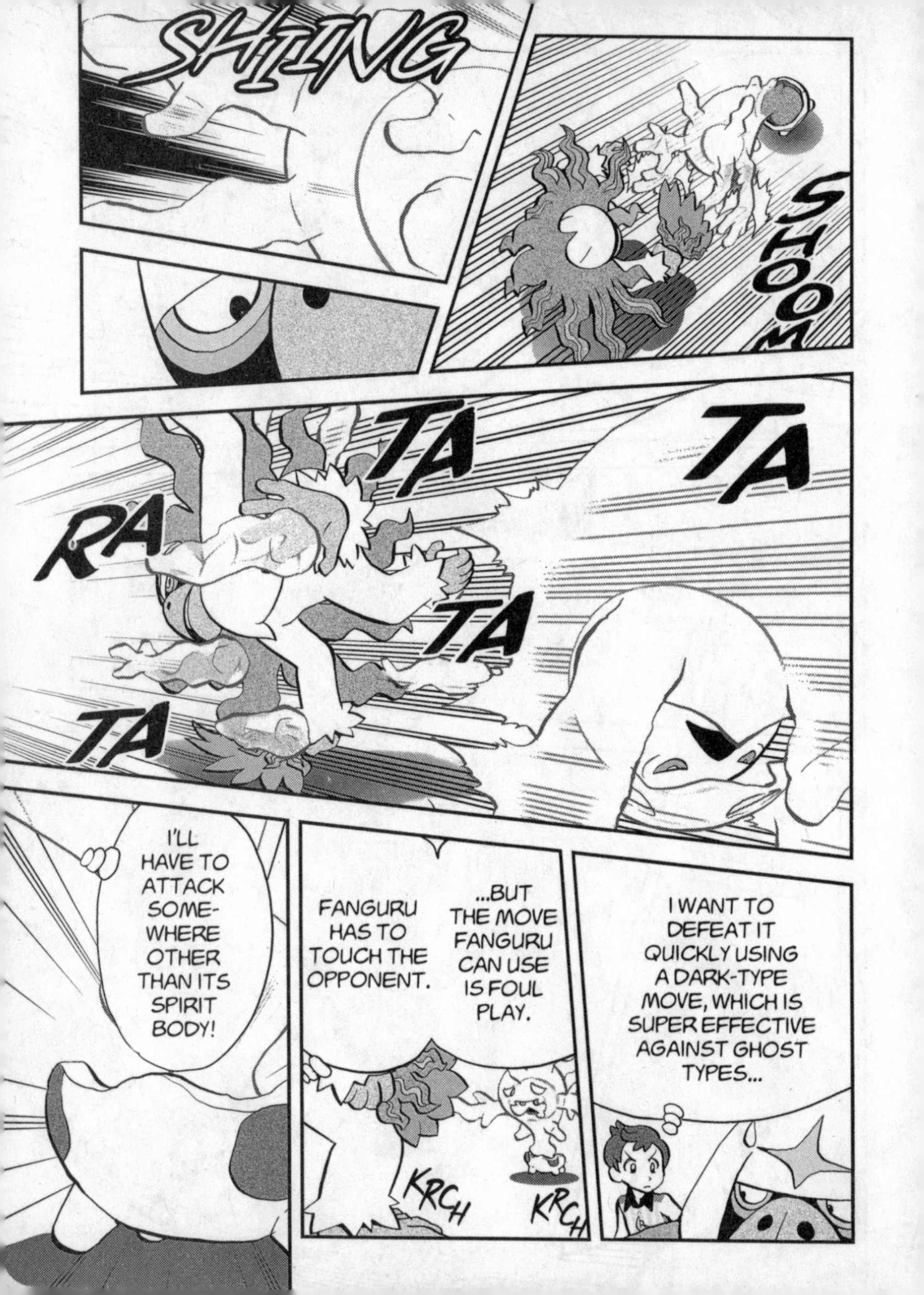
SHOOM
SHING
TA
TA
RA
TA
TA
I WANT TO DEFEAT IT QUICKLY USING A DARK-TYPE MOVE, WHICH IS SUPER EFFECTIVE AGAINST GHOST TYPES...
...BUT THE MOVE FANGURU CAN USE IS FOUL PLAY.
FANGURU HAS TO TOUCH THE OPPONENT.
KRCH
KRCH
I'LL HAVE TO ATTACK SOME-WHERE OTHER THAN ITS SPIRIT BODY!

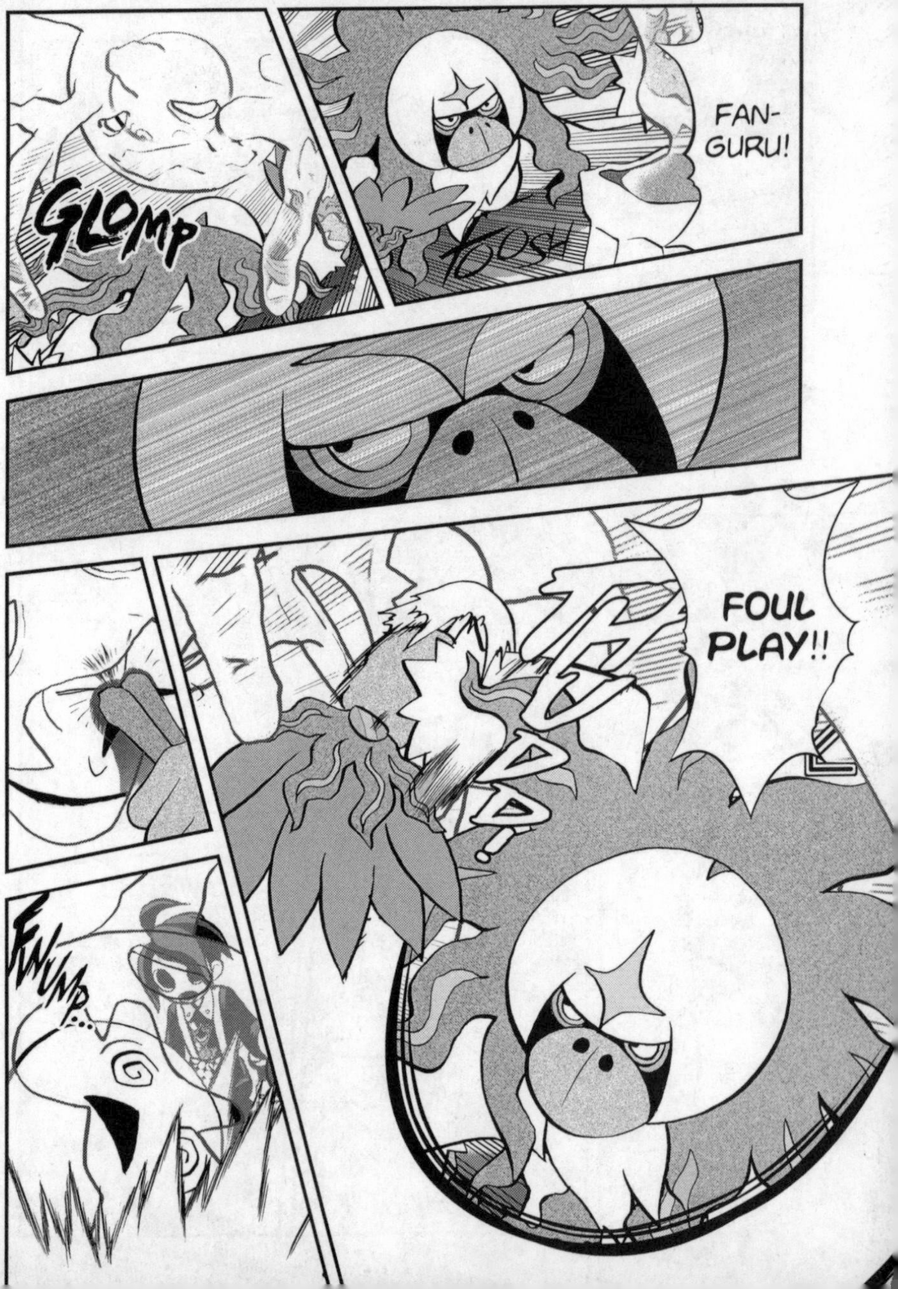
FAN-GURU!
FOOSH
GLOMP
FOUL PLAY!!
FNUMP...

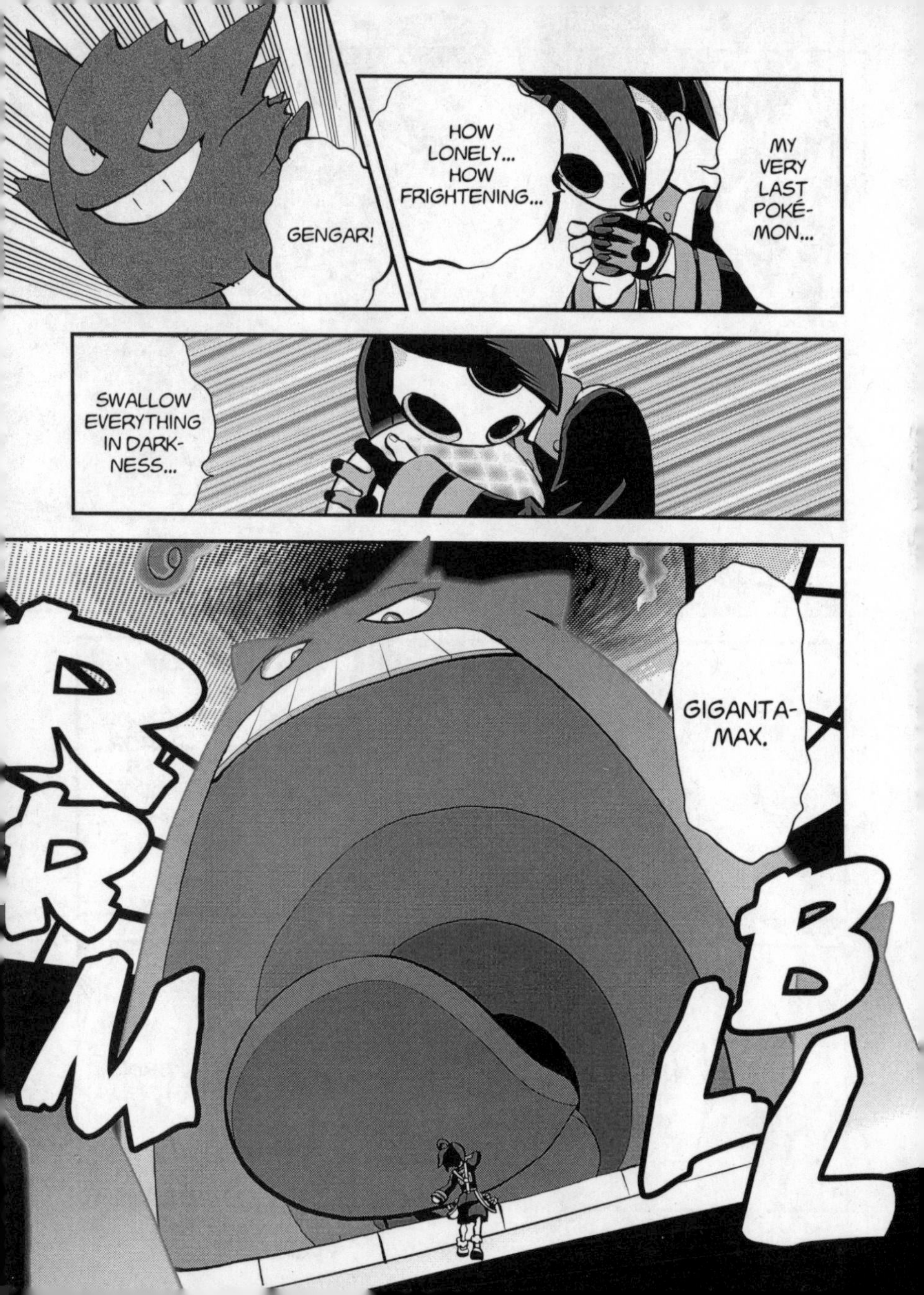
MY VERY LAST POKÉ-MON...
HOW LONELY... HOW FRIGHTENING...
GENGAR!
SWALLOW EVERYTHING IN DARK-NESS...
GIGANTA-MAX.

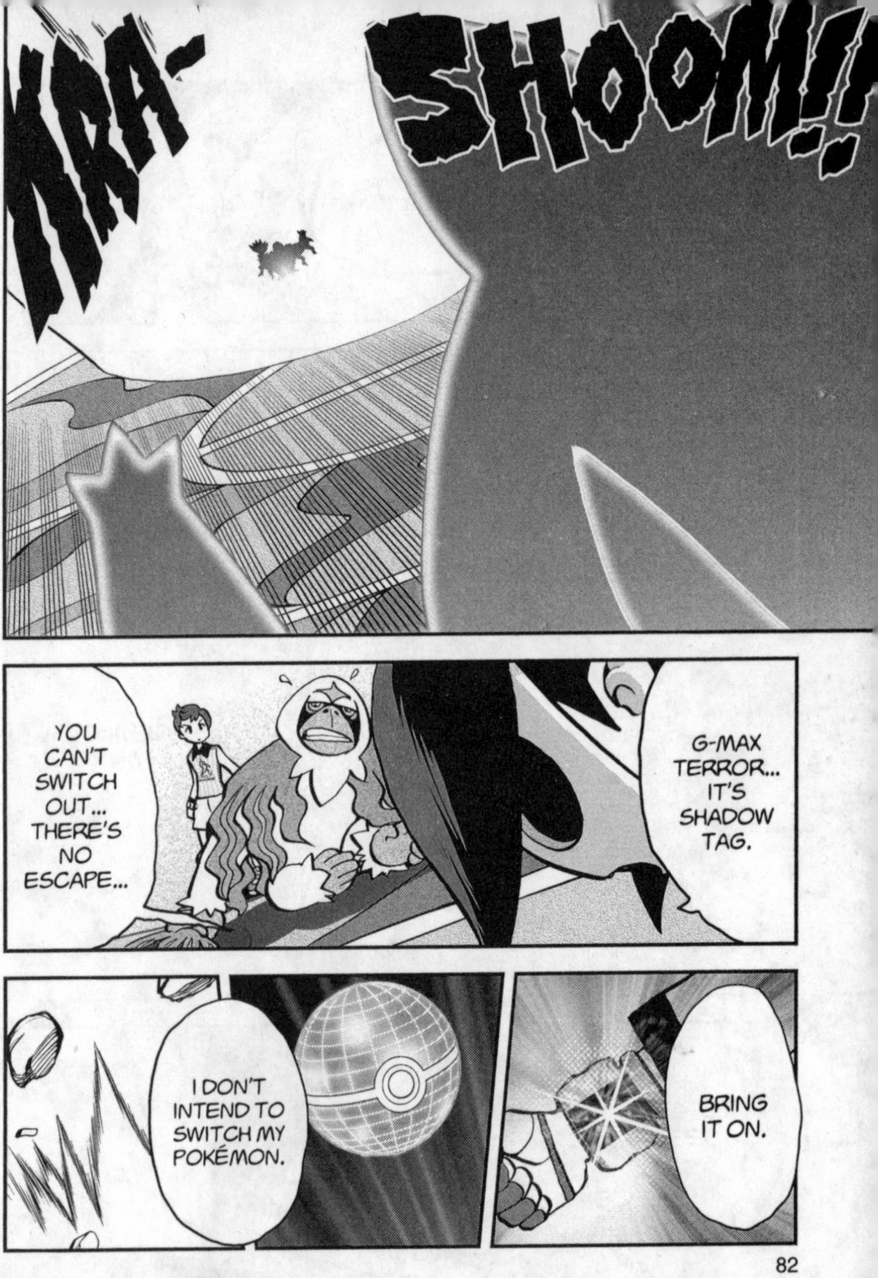
KRA-
SHOOM!!
G-MAX TERROR... IT'S SHADOW TAG.
YOU CAN'T SWITCH OUT... THERE'S NO ESCAPE...
BRING IT ON.
I DON'T INTEND TO SWITCH MY POKÉMON.

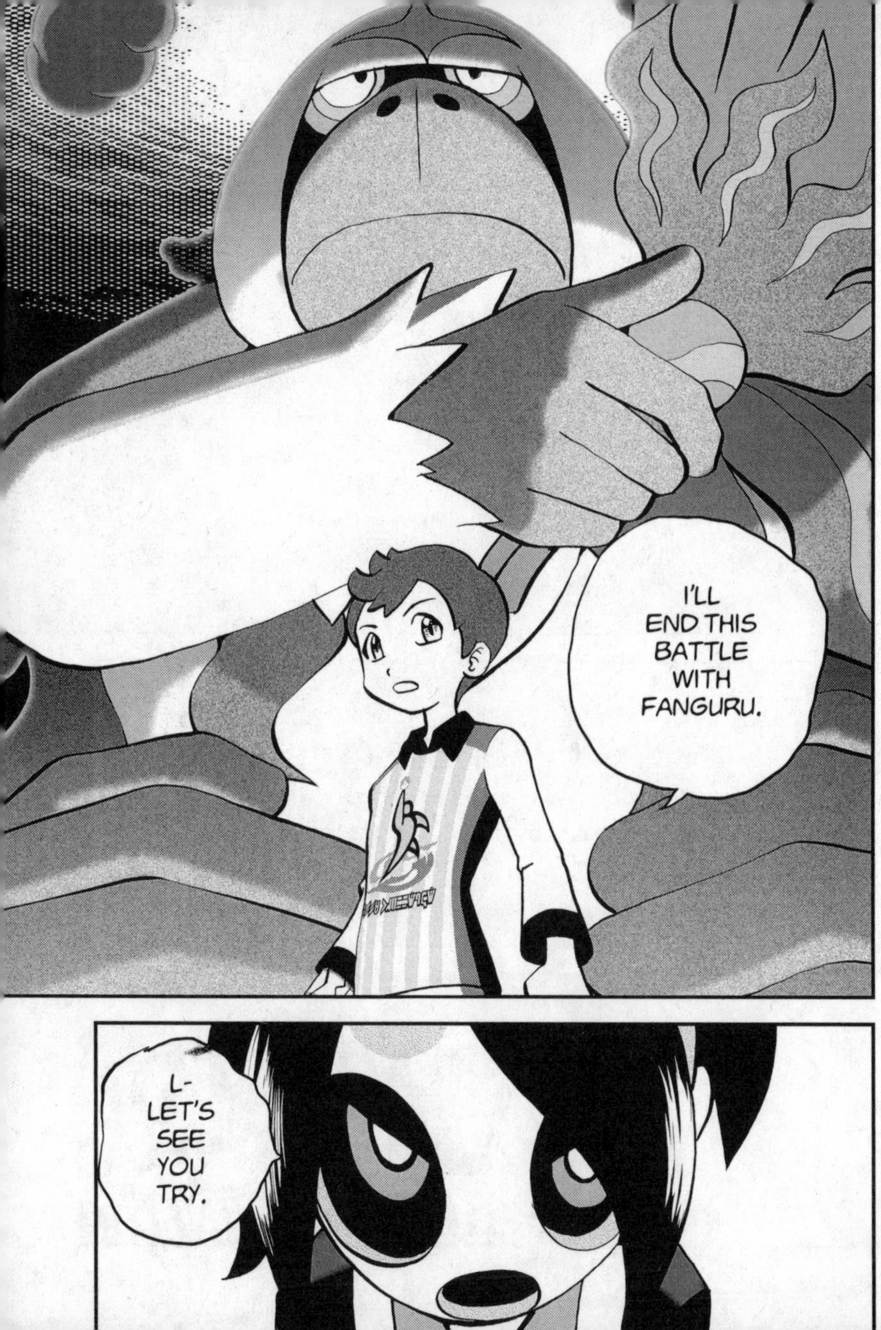
I'LL END THIS BATTLE WITH FANGURU.
L-LET'S SEE YOU TRY.

Pokémon™

Sword & Shield

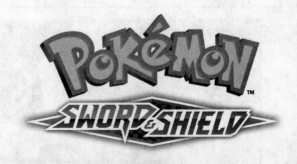

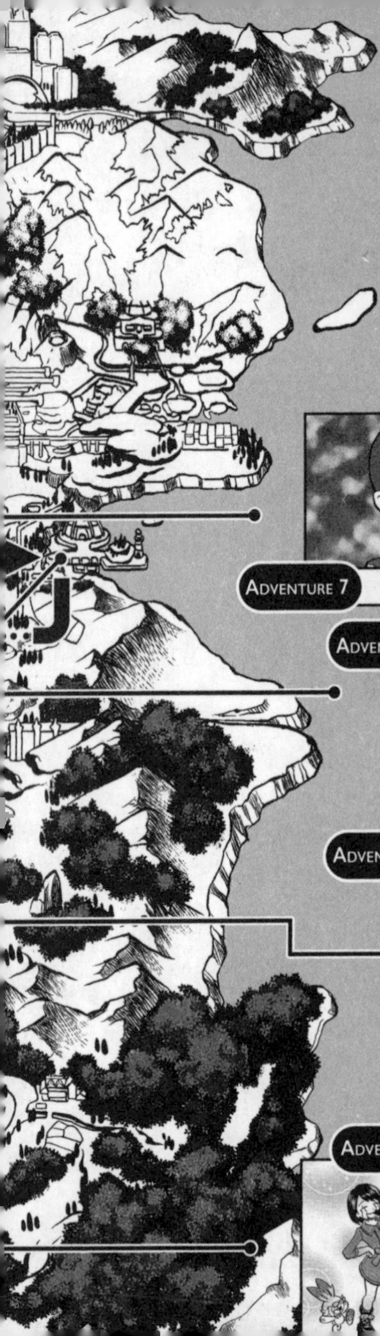

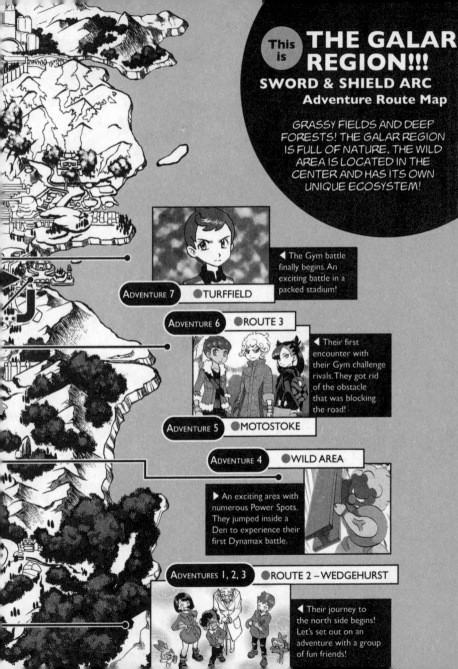

This is THE GALAR REGION!!!

SWORD & SHIELD ARC

Adventure Route Map

GRASSY FIELDS AND DEEP FORESTS! THE GALAR REGION IS FULL OF NATURE. THE WILD AREA IS LOCATED IN THE CENTER AND HAS ITS OWN UNIQUE ECOSYSTEM!

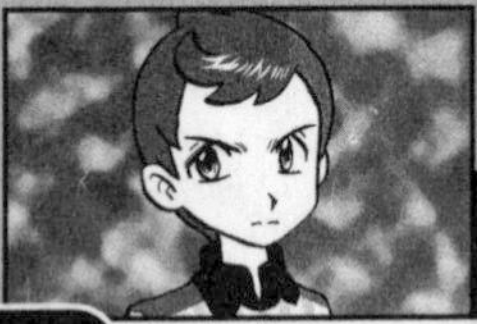

ADVENTURE 7 ● TURFFIELD

◀ The Gym battle finally begins. An exciting battle in a packed stadium!

ADVENTURE 6 ● ROUTE 3

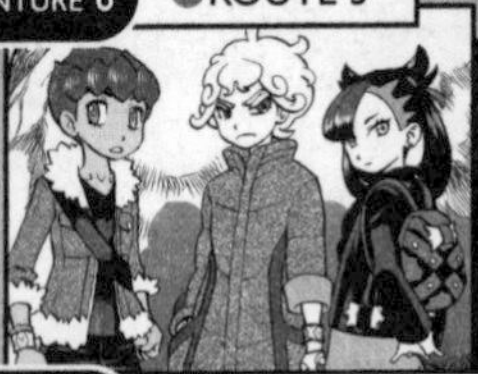

◀ Their first encounter with their Gym challenge rivals. They got rid of the obstacle that was blocking the road!

ADVENTURE 5 ● MOTOSTOKE

ADVENTURE 4 ● WILD AREA

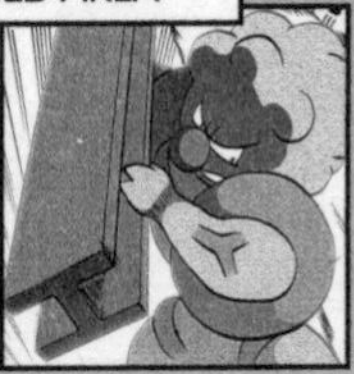

▶ An exciting area with numerous Power Spots. They jumped inside a Den to experience their first Dynamax battle.

ADVENTURES 1, 2, 3 ● ROUTE 2 – WEDGEHURST

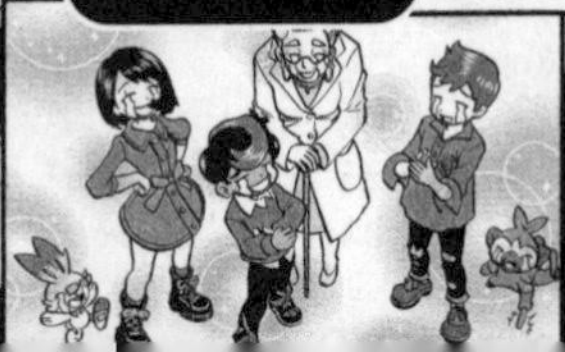

◀ Their journey to the north side begins! Let's set out on an adventure with a group of fun friends!

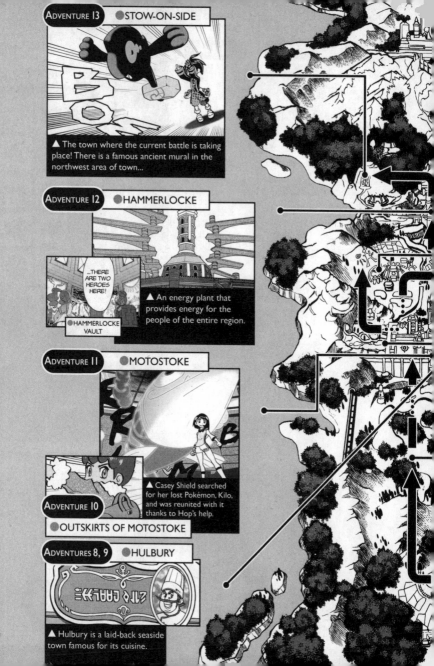

ADVENTURE 13 — STOW-ON-SIDE

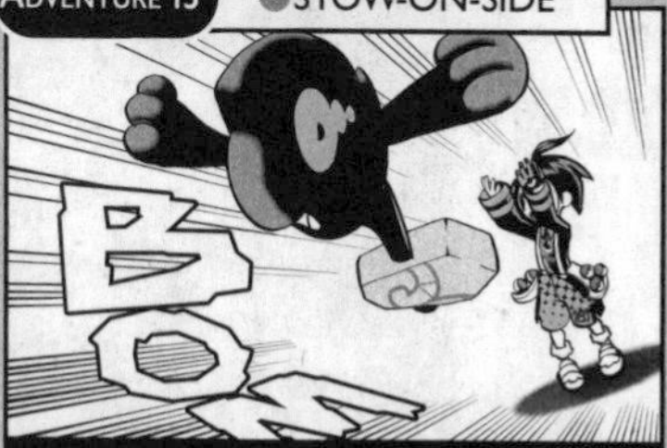

BOOM

▲ The town where the current battle is taking place! There is a famous ancient mural in the northwest area of town...

ADVENTURE 12 — HAMMERLOCKE

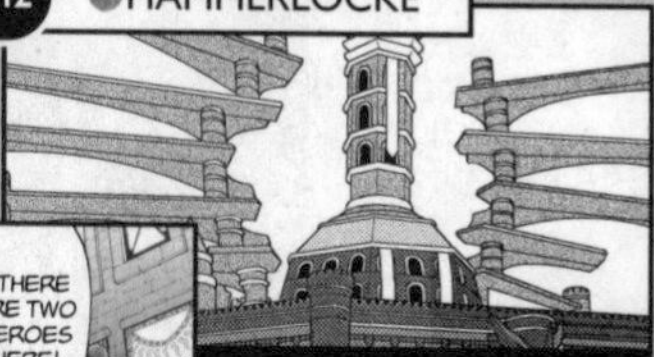

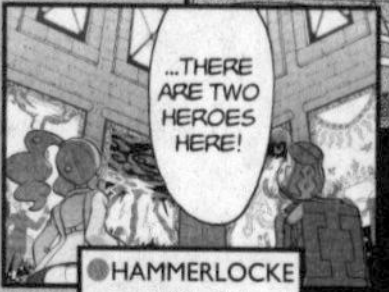

...THERE ARE TWO HEROES HERE!

HAMMERLOCKE VAULT

▲ An energy plant that provides energy for the people of the entire region.

ADVENTURE 11 — MOTOSTOKE

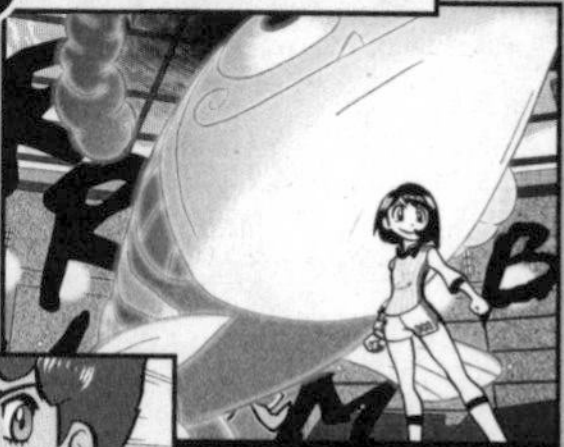

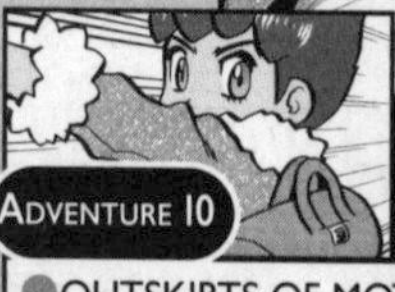

▲ Casey Shield searched for her lost Pokémon, Kilo, and was reunited with it thanks to Hop's help.

ADVENTURE 10 — OUTSKIRTS OF MOTOSTOKE

ADVENTURES 8, 9 — HULBURY

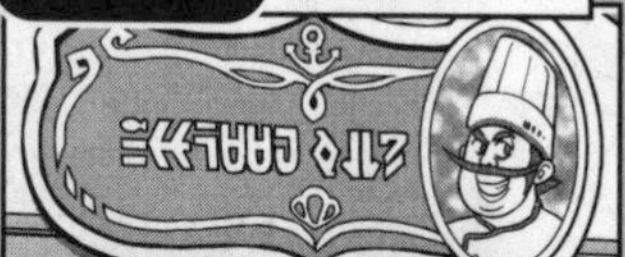

▲ Hulbury is a laid-back seaside town famous for its cuisine.

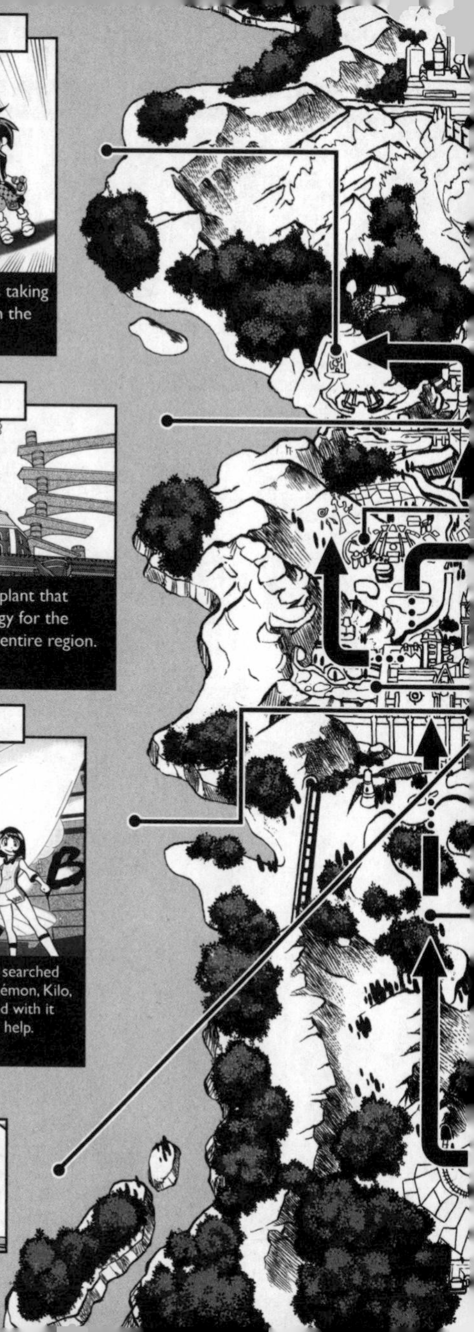

MOTOSTOKE STADIUM **3**	HULBURY STADIUM **2**	TURFFIELD STADIUM **1**

THESE ARE THE 8 MAJOR GYM LEADERS !!!

GALAR REGION

KABU	**NESSA**	**MILO**

SPECIALTY:	SPECIALTY:	SPECIALTY:
FIRE	WATER	GRASS

| KABU'S GYM IS SAID TO BE THE FIRST REAL ROADBLOCK OF THE GYM CHALLENGE, AND MANY CHALLENGERS ARE DEFEATED BY HIM EVERY YEAR!! HIS UNIFORM NUMBER IS 187. | A COMPETITIVE GYM LEADER. HER UNIFORM NUMBER IS 049. SHE IS A VERY BUSY PERSON WHO WORKS AS A MODEL DURING HER FREE TIME! | THE GYM LEADER OF TURFFIELD, A FARMING TOWN. AN EASYGOING PERSON WHOSE MOTTO IS TO ENJOY THE BATTLES. HIS UNIFORM NUMBER IS 831. |

CHAIRMAN ROSE

"THE GYM CHALLENGE IS A POPULAR EVENT WITH TRAINERS AND FANS ALIKE. LET'S MEET THE FORMIDABLE LEADERS WHO AWAIT THE CHALLENGERS!!"

▲ KABU'S CENTISKORCH WAS A PILLAR OF FIRE!

▲ THE OVERWHELMING SIGHT OF THE GIGANTAMAX. WHAT A FIERCE BATTLE!

▲ MILO'S ELDEGOSS WAS A TOUGH OPPONENT.

HAMMERLOCKE STADIUM **8**	SPIKEMUTH STADIUM **7**	CIRCHESTER STADIUM **6**	BALLONLEA STADIUM **5**	STOW-ON-SIDE STADIUM **4**
RAIHAN	**?**	**?**	**OPAL**	**ALLISTER**

SPECIALTY:	SPECIALTY:	SPECIALTY:	SPECIALTY:	SPECIALTY:
DRAGON	?	?	FAIRY	GHOST

LEON'S GREATEST RIVAL, AND A SKILLED TRAINER EVERY BIT THE EQUAL OF THE CHAMPION! HE IS THE FINAL AND GREATEST ROAD-BLOCK WHO PROTECTS THE LAST GYM!!	SPIKEMUTH IS A UNIQUE PLACE WHERE THE ENTIRE TOWN IS INSIDE AN ARCADE. WHO IS THE SEVENTH COMPETITOR THAT AWAITS THE CHALLENGERS IN THIS EERIE, RUN-DOWN TOWN?!	THE SIXTH GYM LEADER AWAITS THE CHALLENGER AT CIRCHESTER, A SNOWY AREA. THIS WILL DEFINITELY BE ONE OF THE IMPORTANT BATTLES IN THE SECOND HALF.	AT 88 YEARS YOUNG, OPAL IS THE OLDEST OF THE GALAR GYM LEADERS. SHE LOVES TO QUIZ HER OPPO-NENTS!	A VERY SHY BOY WHO HIDES HIS FACE WITH A MASK. HE HAS THE POWER TO SEE GHOSTS. HIS UNIFORM NUMBER IS 291, AND HE IS CURRENTLY FIGHTING AGAINST HENRY!!

▲ A POWER-FUL POKÉMON WHOSE ABILITY, SAND SPIT, WILL SUMMON A SANDSTORM!!

"DON'T EXPECT ANY EASY BATTLES!"

...ETARY
...ANA

▲ ITS HORRIFYING TONGUE IS THE ENTRANCE TO THE UNDER-WORLD!!

Hidenori Kusaka is the writer for *Pokémon Adventures*. Running continuously for over 20 years, *Pokémon Adventures* is the only manga series to completely cover all the *Pokémon* games and has become one of the most popular series of all time. In addition to writing manga, he also edits children's books and plans mixed-media projects for Shogakukan's children's magazines. He uses the Pokémon Electrode as his author portrait.

———————————

Satoshi Yamamoto is the artist for *Pokémon Adventures*, which he began working on in 2001, starting with volume 10. Yamamoto launched his manga career in 1993 with the horror-action title *Kimen Senshi*, which ran in Shogakukan's *Weekly Shonen Sunday* magazine, followed by the series *Kaze no Denshosha*. Yamamoto's favorite manga creators/artists include FUJIKO F FUJIO (*Doraemon*), Yukinobu Hoshino (*2001 Nights*), and Katsuhiro Otomo (*Akira*). He loves films, monsters, detective novels, and punk rock music. He uses the Pokémon Swalot as his artist portrait.

Pokémon: Sword & Shield
Volume 4
VIZ Media Edition

Story by HIDENORI KUSAKA
Art by SATOSHI YAMAMOTO

©2022 Pokémon.
©1995–2020 Nintendo / Creatures Inc. / GAME FREAK inc.
TM, ®, and character names are trademarks of Nintendo.
POCKET MONSTERS SPECIAL SWORD SHIELD Vol. 2
by Hidenori KUSAKA, Satoshi YAMAMOTO
© 2020 Hidenori KUSAKA, Satoshi YAMAMOTO
All rights reserved.
Original Japanese edition published by SHOGAKUKAN.
English translation rights in the United States of America, Canada, the United Kingdom,
Ireland, Australia and New Zealand arranged with SHOGAKUKAN.

Original Cover Design—Hiroyuki KAWASOME (grafio)

Translation—Tetsuichiro Miyaki
English Adaptation—Molly Tanzer
Touch-Up & Lettering—Annaliese "Ace" Christman
Cover Color—Philana Chen
Design—Alice Lewis
Editor—Joel Enos

The stories, characters, and incidents mentioned
in this publication are entirely fictional.

Printed in the U.S.A.

Published by VIZ Media, LLC
P.O. Box 77010
San Francisco, CA 94107

10 9 8 7 6 5 4 3 2 1
First printing, August 2022

PARENTAL ADVISORY
POKÉMON: SWORD & SHIELD is rated A
and is suitable for readers of all ages.

viz.com

Coming Next Volume

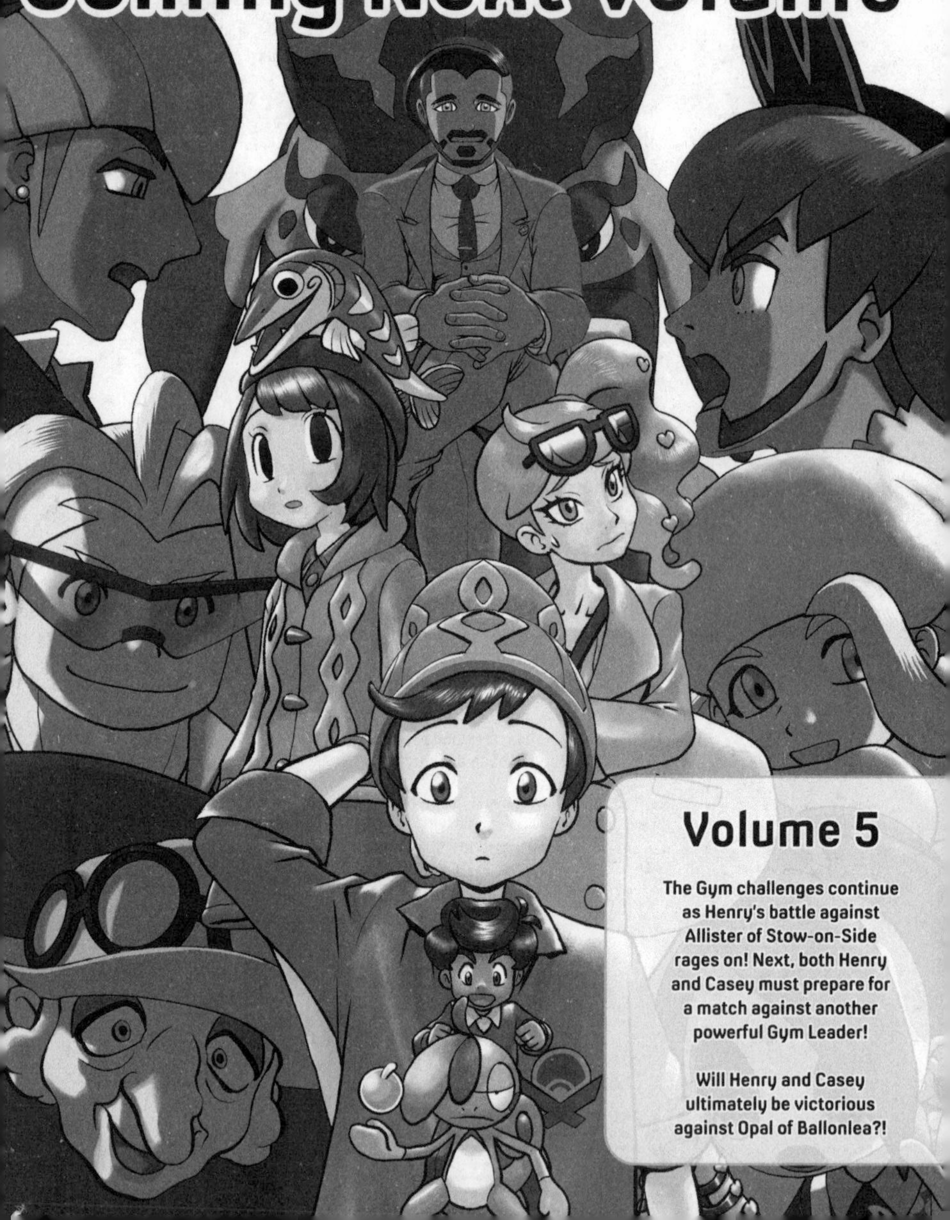

Volume 5

The Gym challenges continue as Henry's battle against Allister of Stow-on-Side rages on! Next, both Henry and Casey must prepare for a match against another powerful Gym Leader!

Will Henry and Casey ultimately be victorious against Opal of Ballonlea?!

ALL YOUR FAVORITE POKÉMON GAME CHARACTERS JUMP OUT OF THE SCREEN INTO THE PAGES OF THIS ACTION-PACKED MANGA!

Pokémon
ADVENTURES™
COLLECTOR'S EDITION
Story by HIDENORI KUSAKA   Art by MATO

A stylish new omnibus edition of the best-selling *Pokémon Adventures* manga, collecting all the original volumes of the series you know and love!

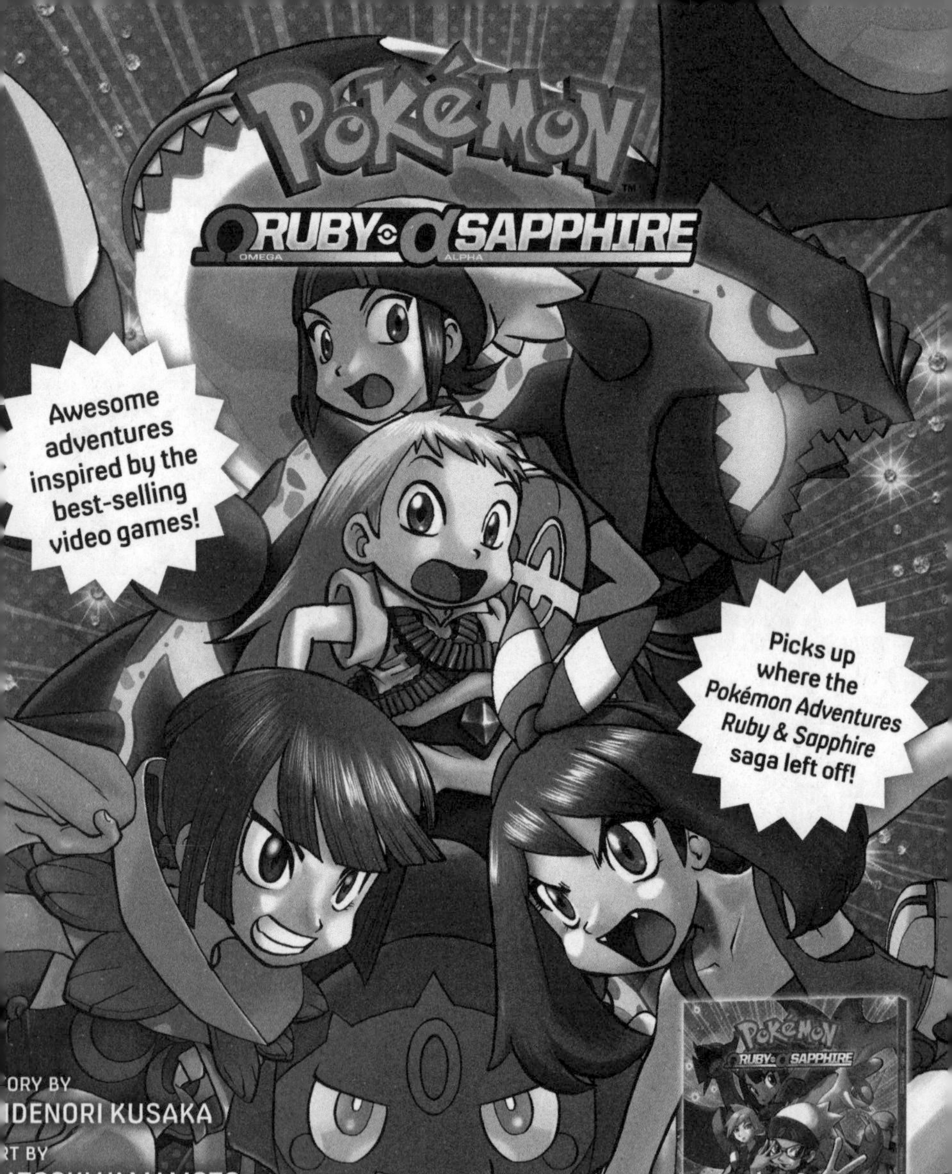
Pokémon
ΩRUBY · αSAPPHIRE
OMEGA ALPHA
Awesome adventures inspired by the best-selling video games!
Picks up where the Pokémon Adventures Ruby & Sapphire saga left off!
ORY BY
IDENORI KUSAKA
T BY
ATOSHI YAMAMOTO

Pokémon

HORIZON
SUN & MOON

Akira's summer vacation in the Alola region heats up when he befriends a Rockruff with a mysterious gemstone. Together, Akira hopes they can achieve his newfound dream of becoming a Pokémon Trainer and master the amazing Z-Move. But first, Akira needs to pass a test to earn a Trainer Passport. This becomes more difficult when Rockruff gets kidnapped! And then Team Kings shows up with—you guessed it—evil plans for world domination!

Story & Art
TENYA YABUNO

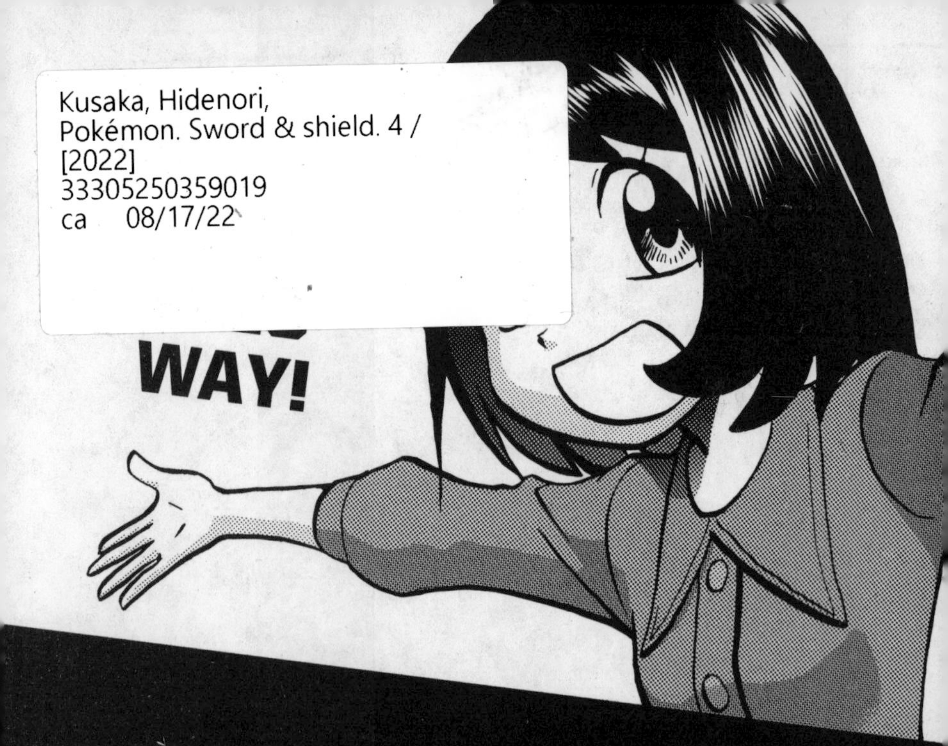
WAY!

THIS IS THE END OF THIS GRAPHIC NOVEL!

To properly enjoy this VIZ Media graphic novel, please turn it around and begin reading from right to left.

This book has been printed in the original Japanese format in order to preserve the orientation of the original artwork. Have fun with it!

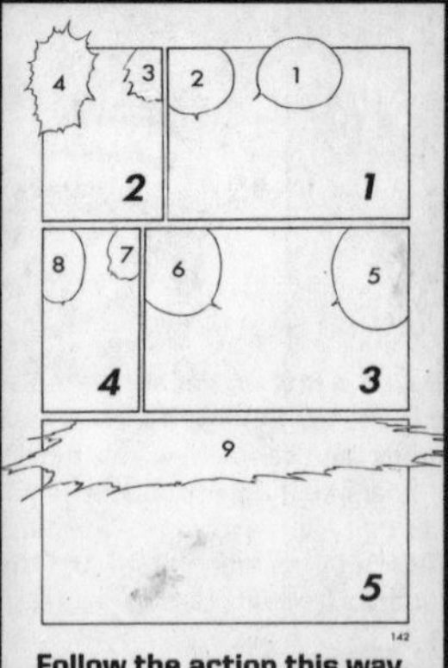

Follow the action this way.